'How old are you

'Twenty-five,' she answered.

He looked grave. 'Old enough to know better, then. Darcy, I realise this can't be easy for you, but what are you doing still staying around Daniel Simon if he's told you he's going to marry someone else?'

She blinked her confusion. 'But he isn't married to her yet...'

Logan gave a groan. 'Darcy, you're an attractive young lady yourself—oh, Darcy...'

Logan's head lowered and his mouth claimed hers.

It was the last thing, the very last thing Darcy had been expecting. But then it came to a sudden end, Logan wrenching his mouth from hers.

'I'm sorry, Darcy. I didn't mean to do that. I brought you here and I almost ended up making love to you. I just—the man is old enough to be your father, for goodness' sake!'

'What man?' Darcy frowned her puzzlement.

'Daniel Simon.'

'I don't seem to have explained, Logan. Daniel Simon *is* my father.'

BACHELOR COUSINS

Three cousins of Scottish descent...
they're male, millionaires and they're marriageable!

Meet Logan, Fergus and Brice, three tall, dark, handsome men about town. They've made their millions in London, but their hearts belong to the heather-clad hills of their Grandfather McDonald's Scottish estate.

Logan, Fergus and Brice are all very intriguing characters. Logan likes his life exactly as it is, and is determined not to change—even for a woman...until scatty, emotional Darcy turns his neatly ordered world upside down! Fergus is clever, witty, laid-back and determined to view things in his own particular way...until the adorably petite Chloe begs him to change his mind—she's willing to pay any price to get him to agree! Finally, there's Brice: tough, resolute and determined, he's accountable to no one...until dark-eyed beauty Sabrina makes him think again!

Logan, Fergus and Brice are about to give up their keenly fought-for bachelor status for three wonderful women—laugh, cry and read all about their trials and tribulations in their pursuit of love.

TO MARRY McKENZIE

BY
CAROLE MORTIMER

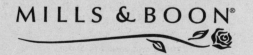

MILLS & BOON®

All the characters in this book have no existence outside the imagination of the author, and have no relation whatsoever to anyone bearing the same name or names. They are not even distantly inspired by any individual known or unknown to the author, and all the incidents are pure invention.

First published in Great Britain 2002
Harlequin Mills & Boon Limited,
Eton House, 18-24 Paradise Road, Richmond, Surrey TW9 1SR

© Carole Mortimer 2002

ISBN 0 263 82923 5

Set in Times Roman 10½ on 12 pt.
01-0402-48054

Printed and bound in Spain
by Litografía Rosés, S.A., Barcelona

CHAPTER ONE

CRASH!

'Damn!'

Logan looked up from the letters he was signing, his expression one of puzzlement as he heard first the crash of what sounded like glass, quickly followed by the expletive.

What—?

Crash!

'Double damn!'

Logan's expression turned to one of bemusement as he put down his pen to stand up, moving in the direction from which the sound of breaking glass was coming: the boardroom that adjoined his vast office.

He and a couple of business associates had lunched in there earlier, discussing contracts while they ate; Logan had found this to be a good way of doing business. The table was still partially set for the meal, he now discovered, but the room itself was empty.

'Damn and blast it,' a disembodied voice muttered impatiently. 'That's two glasses I'll have to replace now. I— ouch!' The last was obviously a cry of pain.

Logan was even more intrigued now, walking slowly around the long mahogany table, to find himself peering down at the top of a head of bright red hair. Ah, the puzzle was solved: this was the girl—woman?—who had served their lunch to them, an employee of Chef Simon. Logan hadn't taken too much notice of her during the meal, having been intent on his business discussions, b

5

remember the occasional glimpse of that gleaming red hair as she'd moved quietly round the table.

The girl straightened, frowning down at her left hand, where a considerable amount of blood had appeared at the end of one of her fingers.

'Did you cut yourself?'

Whatever reaction Logan had expected to his sympathetic query, it was not to have the girl jump almost six inches in the air in her nervousness, knocking over one of the water glasses as she did so!

Logan managed to reach out and catch the glass before it rolled off the table—to join the two he could see now were already shattered on the shiny wood-tiled floor.

'No point in your having to buy three replacements instead of two,' he murmured dryly as he righted the glass on the table. 'Is it a bad cut?' He reached out with the intention of looking at the girl's hand.

Only to have that hand snatched out of his grasp as it was hidden behind her back. The girl looked up at him with stricken grey eyes. 'I'm so sorry if I've disturbed you, Mr McKenzie,' she gasped. 'I was just clearing away, and—and—I broke the glasses.' She looked down at the shattered pieces. 'And—and—' Whatever she had been about to say was lost as she suddenly dissolved into floods of tears.

Logan recoiled from this display of emotion, frowning darkly. 'Hey, it's only a couple of glasses. I'm sure Chef Simon isn't that much of an ogre that you have to cry about it.'

The outside catering company of Chef Simon had been taking care of the occasional business lunches Logan had in his boardroom for over a year now, and Logan had always found the other man reasonable to deal with. Although he hadn't seen this young girl before, so perhaps she was new, and feared losing her job because of those breakages…?

'You could always tell Chef Simon that I broke them,' he attempted to cajole; weeping women were not his forte!

Well…not when they were weeping because they were worried or upset, he acknowledged ruefully as he remembered that last meeting with Gloria a couple of weeks ago. The frown deepened on his brow as he recalled the tears she had cried, tears of anger and frustration because he had told her their year-long relationship was over. She had even thrown a vase of flowers at him when he'd refused to change his mind, Logan remembered with distaste.

'Oh, I couldn't do that,' the girl instantly refused. 'Then he would put it on your bill, and that wouldn't be fair at all.' She shook her head.

Fair… It wasn't a word Logan heard too often, either in business or his personal life. Besides, the cost of a couple of glasses would hardly bankrupt his multimillion-pound, multifaceted company…

The girl reached up to wipe away the tears staining her face, inadvertently smearing blood over her cheeks instead. 'Oh, damn,' she muttered frustratedly as she realised what she had done, searching unsuccessfully in the pockets of her trousers for a tissue.

'You like that word, don't you?' Logan murmured, his head tilted as he looked at her properly for the first time.

She was a tiny little thing, barely reaching up to his shoulders, black trousers and a cream blouse emphasising the slenderness of her body, that shoulder-length bright red hair framing a face that, at first glance, seemed to be covered in freckles. On second glance, he saw the freckles only covered her cheeks and nose; her grey eyes framed by thick dark lashes, her mouth wide, unsmiling at the moment, her chin pointed d

Not exactly—

Where had that smile come from? Logan wondered dazedly as he found himself instantly reassessing the opinion he had just formed of this girl's looks being unremarkable. When she smiled, as she was doing now, those grey eyes became darkly luminous, dimples appeared in the slightly rounded cheeks, her teeth shone white and even in a softly alluring mouth.

Logan stared at her uncomprehendingly; he felt as if he had just had all the breath knocked out of his body!

'It's better than a lot of the alternatives,' she acknowledged. 'And, while I appreciate your offer concerning the glasses…' the girl continued to smile, appearing to have no idea of the effect she had just had on him '…as you said, it's not worth getting upset about,' she dismissed with a shrug.

'Then whatever were you crying about?' Logan rasped, angry with himself—and her!—for his unprecedented reaction just now.

The smile faded—and so did Logan's confusion. He shook his head. The girl was plain, for goodness' sake; just a load of freckles and smoky grey eyes!

'Well?' he snapped impatiently.

She was looking up at him reproachfully with those wide grey eyes now. 'I—I—I've cut myself!' She held up the damaged finger.

Logan scowled down at it. 'It appears to have stopped bleeding.' Which it had. 'And it doesn't look too serious.' Which it didn't.

And, he decided irritably, he had already wasted enough of his afternoon on this situation—whatever it might be!

'I'll have my secretary bring through a plaster,' he bit out abruptly. 'In the meantime, I would suggest you give that finger a wash. And your face,' he added with an impatient glance at her bloodstained cheek.

She put a hand up self-consciously to her cheek. 'I said I'm sorry for disturbing you.' She frowned, looking on the verge of tears once again.

She could have no idea how—momentarily!—she had disturbed him!

'What's your name?' he asked.

'Darcy,' she said miserably.

'Well, Miss Darcy—'

'Darcy is my first name,' she corrected, even as she sniffed inelegantly.

Oh, no, she was going to cry again! And wasn't Darcy a boy's name...?

'Your father wanted a son, hmm?' Logan murmured mockingly.

Those grey eyes flashed angrily. 'What he wanted, and what he got, are two entirely different things,' she clipped.

'It usually is where women are concerned,' Logan drawled derisively.

Darcy looked up at him beneath those long, dark lashes. 'Are you married, Mr McKenzie?'

Logan's surprised brows shot up beneath the dark hair that fell lightly over his brow. What did his married state have to do with anything?

'As it happens—no,' he answered slowly.

She nodded—as if she had already guessed as much. 'Women, I've invariably found, often respond in character to the men they are involved with. For example—'

'Darcy, I believe you were here to serve a meal and then depart, not to psychoanalyse the client!' Logan cut in scathingly, his jaw tightly clenched.

Until a few minutes ago he had been quietly pleased with his day; lunch had been a success, contracts were being drawn up even as he spoke to this young lady, and he had been looking forward to having dinner this evening with a beautiful blonde he had met at a dinner party on Saturday. That sense of well-being had now been lost in an increasing desire to strangle this young woman!

Darcy looked slightly flustered. 'I'm so sorry. I—It's just—I—I'm really not myself today!' she choked before burying her face in her hands as the tears began to fall once more.

Logan shook his head dazedly, once again feeling totally out of his depth in the face of the renewed tears. 'Oh, for goodness' sake!' he muttered before reaching out and taking her into his arms.

She felt so tiny as he cradled her against the hardness of his chest, that red hair feeling like silk against his fingers as he absently caressed it, her shoulder-blades so fragile to his touch she was like a little bird—

What on earth was he doing? This was the waitress who had come to serve lunch, for heaven's sake! More to the point, anyone could walk in on them and completely misconstrue the situation!

He shifted uncomfortably. 'Er—Darcy…?'

Her only answer to his tentative query was to bury her face even further into his shirt-front, the dampness of the material clinging to his chest now.

Logan felt totally out of his depth, beginning to wish that someone *would* come in and interrupt them—whatever construction was put on his actions!

'Here,' he prompted gruffly, handing her the snowy white handkerchief from his breast pocket, relieved when she moved away from him slightly to give her nose a good blow.

No wonder not too many women cried in his presence, he decided ruefully, if Darcy's unattractive appearance was anything to go by—she looked like a startled fawn: all eyes and blotchy cheeks!

'I really am so sorry,' she said miserably. 'It's just that I had some—rather disturbing news, earlier, before coming out. I don't usually cry all over perfect strangers, I can assure you.' She gave a watery smile.

Logan gave the ghost of a smile in return. 'That's okay—I'm far from perfect!' he attempted to tease, wondering exactly what sort of news this young woman could have received to reduce her to this state. 'Is it anything I can help you with?' he heard himself offer—and then frowned at this uncharacteristic interest in a stranger's—perfect or otherwise!—predicament.

Having originated from a large, Scottish-based family—consisting of his aged grandfather, his mother, a couple of aunts and numerous cousins—Logan usually found it all too easy to distance himself from the upsets that seemed to constantly plague his family. If he didn't he would spend most of his time caught up in one intrigue or another, and he preferred a much quieter life than that. Which was why he spent the majority of his time at his London apartment!

Why he should be showing this interest in the problems of a complete stranger he had no idea—especially one who had cried all over him and left bloodstains on his shirt!

Darcy's smile was slightly bitter. 'I doubt it.' She shook her head. 'But thank you for asking.'

He felt irritated because she wouldn't tell him what was bothering her! What on earth was wrong with him?

'A problem shared is a problem halved, so they say,' he encouraged cajolingly.

'I doubt you would be interested.' She shook her head again, beginning to look decidedly embarrassed now.

'Try me,' Logan prompted huskily.

Darcy shrugged again. 'It's just that— No, I really can't,' she decided firmly. 'Da—Chef Simon,' she corrected awkwardly, 'wouldn't appreciate it if he knew I had been discussing his personal life with one of his customers,' she admitted.

Chef Simon? *Daniel* Simon…? For surely this young woman had been going to call the renowned chef by his first name? And if her tears were anything to go by, it was a liberty that implied a much more intimate relationship between them than just that of employer and employee.

Daniel Simon and this girl, Darcy?

Logan couldn't hide his surprise. This girl looked no older than her early twenties at most, whereas from what Logan knew of Daniel Simon he was a man in his early fifties. Spring and Autumn. Not that it was an unusual arrangement, Logan acknowledged, he had just never thought of the other man in that particular light. In fact, he couldn't say he had given a single thought to Daniel Simon's private life!

As he didn't want to think about it now, either! 'You're probably right.' Logan nodded tersely. 'I'll send Karen through with the plaster,' he added dismissively before turning to leave.

'Mr McKenzie…?'

He turned reluctantly. 'Yes, Darcy?' he replied warily.

'Thank you,' she told him huskily, smiling at him for the second time today.

Once again causing that numbing jolt in his chest!

The quicker he got out of here, Logan decided grimly, the better! 'You're welcome,' he bit out harshly, making good his escape to the adjoining office this time.

Escape? he questioned himself once he was seated back behind his desk. From the woman Darcy? Ridiculous. He had just had enough of a woman's tears for one day—

especially as she had probably completely ruined his silk shirt with those tears and the blood from her cut finger!

What must Logan McKenzie think of her? Darcy groaned inwardly.

She had tried so hard to keep her worrying thoughts at bay this morning, concentrating on serving lunch to the client and his guests. But she just hadn't been able to control her chaotic thoughts once she'd started to clear away, and dropping the two glasses had seemed like the final straw on a day when she'd already felt as if the bottom were dropping out of her world.

But even so, she really shouldn't have cried all over Logan McKenzie's pristine white silk shirt. She very much doubted he would be able to remove those bloodstains!

She still had his sodden handkerchief, she realised as she looked down with dismay at the screwed-up item in her hand. Not that she could have given it back to him in this condition; she would have to launder it first and send it back to him. Not that she thought Logan McKenzie would miss one white handkerchief; it was just a matter of principle.

She—

'Here we are,' announced a bright female voice as Karen Hill, Logan McKenzie's private secretary, came into the room, laden down with disinfectant cream and plasters. 'Logan says you've had an accident.' She looked at Darcy enquiringly.

Logan—Darcy was sure—thought she was one big accident! She cringed with embarrassment now as she remembered the way she had sobbed all over the poor man.

'It's nothing,' she dismissed. 'Just a plaster will be fine ' she accepted lightly, the cut no longer bleeding, alth it stung slightly.

But not as much as remembering her complete breakdown in front of Logan McKenzie a few minutes ago! The sooner she got away from here, the better.

'Thanks.' She accepted the offered plaster. 'Er—do you have any idea of Logan's—Mr McKenzie's,' she corrected awkwardly, 'shirt size?'

Karen's blonde brows shot up in obvious surprise. 'Logan's shirt size…?' she repeated speculatively.

Mistake, Darcy, she admonished herself. If she intended replacing Logan McKenzie's ruined silk shirt she would just have to find another way of finding out what size to purchase.

'It doesn't matter,' she told the other woman brightly, avoiding Karen's questioning gaze as she put the plaster on her finger. 'I'll just finish clearing away here and be on my way,' she added.

'Fine,' the other woman answered distractedly, obviously still puzzled by Darcy's earlier question.

Well, she would have to remain puzzled, Darcy decided irritably; she had already embarrassed herself enough for one day!

Once on her own she cleared away in double-quick fashion, stacking everything into the baskets she had brought up with her, even the broken glass was swept up and wrapped in newspaper for her to take away with her.

It was just her luck to find Logan McKenzie waiting for the ascending lift when she struggled down the corridor with the two laden baskets!

He turned to glance at her, doing a double take as he obviously recognised her, a frown instantly darkening his brow.

Not surprising really, Darcy acknowledged with an inward wince; the poor man was probably wondering whether it would be safe to get into the lift with her, or if

there was a chance it would break down the moment the
doors closed behind the two of them!

'Hello,' she greeted inanely.

'Darcy.' He nodded tersely, glancing impatiently at the
lights indicating the slow ascent of the lift.

Couldn't wait to get away from her, Darcy realised self-
derisively, knowing he would probably make a point of
asking Daniel Simon for her *not* to wait on one of his
business lunches ever again! Well, he needn't worry on
that score; she was only here today because they were
short-staffed.

The restaurant, Chef Simon, opened in London by
Daniel Simon five years ago, had become such a success
that the customers often asked him if he was able to cater
for dinner and luncheon parties in their own homes. The
outside catering company of Chef Simon was a direct result of those requests. With numerous pre-bookings, already six months ahead in some cases, this secondary business was obviously doing very nicely, thank you!

Unfortunately several of the staff were off with flu at
the moment, which was the reason Darcy had been roped
in to help today. At the last disastrous half-hour, she
wished she me.' An impatient Logan McKenzie reached

'He relieved her of one of the heavy baskets.

Darcy blinked her surprise, having been taken unawares,
lost in thought as she was. 'Thank you,' she murmured
dazedly. 'But there's really no need,' she added awkwardly, moving to take the basket back out of his grasp.

Something he obviously had no intention of letting her
do as his long, tapered fingers tightened about the wicker
handle. 'Leave it,' he snapped impatiently as the lift finally
arrived, standing back to allow her to enter first.

Darcy looked at him beneath lowered lash-

pressed the lift button for the ground floor. Aged about thirty-five, he was incredibly good-looking—in an arrogantly austere way, she decided slowly. His short dark hair was straight and silky, blue eyes the colour of the clear Mediterranean Sea, his nose slightly long, sculptured mouth unsmiling now, although Darcy had witnessed several charming smiles during the serving of lunch, his chin squarely firm. Tall and ruggedly muscular, he looked as if he would be more at home on a farm, than in an office wearing tailored suits and silk shirts.

Silk shirts…she remembered with an inward groan, the marks of her crying earlier clearly showing on the now-dried material. She really doubted that the traces of blood on the white silk would come off during dry-cleaning, either.

Darcy was relieved when the lift reached the ground floor, having found the silence between them uncomfortable, to say the least. 'Thanks.' She reached to take the basket from him, making no effort to follow him out of the lift.

Logan McKenzie stood in the doorway to stop the doors closing behind him, frowning again. 'Where are you going?'

'To the basement,' she told him lightly, 've the van parked down there.'

'In that case…' He stepped back into the lift, the instantly closing behind him as he pressed the button marked 'basement'.

'There's really no need,' she told him once again, completely flustered at having the owner of this world-renowned company helping her in this way.

'There's every need,' he rasped grimly. 'A little thing like you shouldn't be carrying these heavy baskets. And correct me if I'm mistaken, but was there only you dealing with the preparation and serving of lunch today?' Logan continued firmly, completely ignoring the fact that she had been about to protest at being called a 'little thing', blue eyes narrowed questioningly.

'Yes.' Darcy shifted the heavy basket to her other hand. 'We're short-staffed today, you see and—'

'No, I don't see,' Logan interrupted shortly, stepping out into the darkened basement that acted as a car park for the office staff of McKenzie Industries. 'Short-staffed or not, you shouldn't have been expected to deal with it all alone. A fact I will be passing on to Daniel Simon at the earliest opportunity,' he added grimly.

'Oh, don't do that!' Darcy turned from loading the van to protest, two wings of embarrassed colour in her cheeks. 'I managed just fine. You had no complaints about lunch, did you?' she pressed determinedly as Logan McKenzie still looked grim.

'No...' he answered slowly.   she assured him

'Then there's no problem   ingly. 'You know, Darcy,' he brightly.   might find Daniel Simon less of a—

He looked   weren't so eager to please.'

He looked up at him, but the subdued lighting in the park made it impossible to read his expression clearly. Which was a pity—because she had no idea what he was talking about!

'It was only a lunch,' she responded, ready to leave now, the van loaded, the keys in her hand.

'I wasn't particularly alluding to lunch,' he rasped.

Then what was he talking about? Admittedly, she could have handled the latter part of this booking with a bit detachment—in fact, a lot more!—but there been nothing wrong with the lunch this man and his guests had been served before her tearful outburst.

Logan McKenzie scowled at her slightly bewildered expression. 'I'm merely offering you some advice from a male point of view, Darcy,' he replied. 'It's up to you whether or not you choose to take it,' he ended abruptly, obviously impatient to be gone now.

'I— Thank you,' Darcy mumbled, having no idea what advice she had just been given!

It wasn't a question of being eager to please where Daniel Simon was concerned; she hadn't really been given too much of an opportunity to do anything else where this lunch today was concerned. She was upset, yes, in fact she was more than upset, but it would have been churlish to refuse to help out when they were short-staffed. Business was business, after all, she acknowledged slightly bitterly.

Logan McKenzie nodded tersely before turning quickly on his heel and striding back to the still-waiting lift, stepping inside, his expression still grim as the doors closed.

What a strange man, Darcy decided as she got into the van and drove out of the car park. Kind one minute, impatient the next, then offering advice—although anyone less like a father-figure, she decided lightly as she imagine!

Oh, well, she decided lightly as she drove through the early-afternoon London traffic, Logan McKenzie was the least of her problems at the moment.

A frown marred the creaminess of her brow as she thought of what was her biggest problem.

Daniel Simon. *Chef* Simon.

And the fact that this morning he had calmly informed her that he intended marrying a woman he had only met for the first time three weeks ago!

CHAPTER TWO

'THIS has just been delivered for you,' Logan's secretary informed him, before placing a large square parcel on top of his desk, his name and the office address clearly printed in black ink on the brown wrapping paper.

Logan looked up with a frown, his thoughts still on the contract he had been studying; the legalese in these things became more complicated by the day. His legal team could obviously deal with it, but he would have liked his cousin Fergus's opinion too before anything was signed.

But his cousin's housekeeper had informed Logan that Fergus had gone to Scotland, to the home of their shared maternal grandfather. No doubt Hugh McDonald had a good reason for appropriating the services of the family lawyer, but, at this precise moment, Logan had little patience for those reasons!

He laid down the gold pen he had been using to mark his way down the pages, running one of his hands over the tiredness of his brow. Yesterday evening, spent with the blonde from Saturday night, had not been the success he had hoped it would be.

In fact, after only half an hour spent alone in the beautiful Andrea's company, he had already discovered that she giggled like a schoolgirl, talked incessantly, mostly about her modelling career, ate almost nothing, because of her figure—whatever that might mean!—and drank even less, for the same reason.

The evening had dragged on interminably for Logan and he had breathed a sigh of relief when he'd finally h able to drop Andrea off at her apartment shortly before midnight. Without asking to see her again!

'What is it?' he prompted Karen now, glancing uninterestedly at the parcel she had put on his desk.

'I have no idea,' his competent secretary told him truthfully. 'I haven't opened it; it's marked "Private and Personal",' she pointed out, with a speculative rise of blonde brows.

Logan's mouth twisted wryly as he surveyed the paper-wrapped parcel. 'Have you checked it isn't a bomb? Or worse,' he drawled dryly, Gloria's shouted threats of 'you'll regret this' still ringing in his ears even after the passing of over two weeks.

Karen grinned, well aware, Logan was sure, that the telephone calls from Miss Granger had ceased two weeks ago. And was obviously totally unsympathetic to Logan's discomfort. Although that wasn't so surprising, Logan accepted ruefully; Karen had worked for him for almost ten years now, had seen several Glorias come and go in his life—and knew that he had remained unaffected by any of them.

'It was hand-delivered by a very reputable courier company,' she assured him teasingly.

He grimaced. 'That's no guarantee!'

Karen laughed softly. 'Go on, Logan, live dangerously for once, and open it.'

He frowned slightly at that 'for once' Karen had tacked onto her teasing statement. Perhaps his life did seem rather predictable to someone outside looking in, but that was the way he liked it. The way he deliberately organised it. Basically because he could remember far too many upsets and emotional scenes when he was a child to tolerate them in his own adult life...

He eyed the parcel once again before picking it up and

turning it over; no return address written on the back. 'Did the courier say who the parcel was from?' He frowned. It wasn't a very heavy parcel; in fact it felt so light it didn't seem as if there was anything inside the box...

'Nope,' Karen answered with a grimace. 'But if you really think it might be a bomb, do you want me to get Gerard to take it down to the basement and—?'

'No, I don't,' Logan assured her dryly. 'To both suggestions,' he added.

'Well, aren't you going to open it?' Karen prompted after several more long seconds had passed.

Logan sat back in his chair, the box still held in his hand as he looked across at her with narrowed blue eyes. 'I bet you were one of those little girls who crept down in the middle of the night on Christmas Eve and opened all her presents before anyone else had even thought of waking up!' he taunted softly.

'And I bet you were one of those infuriating little boys who opened each present slowly, barely ripping the paper, playing with each new toy before moving on to the next parcel!' Karen obviously felt stung into snapping back.

Logan gave an inclination of his head, smiling slightly. 'It seems we would both win our bets,' he said softly. 'You know, Karen, you aren't painting a very impulsive picture of me, either in the past or now!'

An embarrassed flush darkened her cheeks. 'I'm sorry, Logan,' She shook her head. 'I realise it's your parcel—'

'And I'm going to open it. Right now.' He grinned across at her. 'I was only teasing you, Karen,' he told her, even as he methodically unwrapped the brown paper from the parcel, opening up the box beneath to fold back the tissue paper. 'What the—?' He stared uncomprehendingly at the white handkerchief and white silk shirt that lay in the box.

Karen, looking over his shoulder at the contents, whistled softly between her teeth. 'So that's why she wanted to know your shirt size...' she mused.

Logan glanced up at her sharply. 'Who wanted to know?' he rasped.

But he already knew! The white silk shirt, well...with this particular label, that could have been an expensively extravagant present from any woman. But not the laundered white handkerchief. That could only have come from one woman—Darcy!

A quick glance before he folded back the tissue paper and put the lid back on the box showed him there was no accompanying letter inside. But there didn't need to be one; he was in no doubt whatsoever who had sent him these things. While he accepted that the handkerchief was his, and it was very kind of Darcy to launder it and return it to him, he had no intention of accepting the replacement white silk shirt. The girl was a waitress for goodness' sake, and he knew exactly how much a silk shirt of that particular label would have cost her.

His expression was grim as he glanced at his wristwatch: two-thirty. The restaurant would still be open. He glanced up at Karen. 'Could you get me the Chef Simon restaurant on the telephone, please?' he requested tautly.

'Of course.' Karen nodded, moving towards the door. She paused as she opened it. 'Be gentle with her, hmm?' she encouraged. 'She seemed terribly sweet, and—'

'Just get me the number, Karen,' Logan bit out impatiently. The last thing he needed was for his secretary to think Darcy had some sort of crush on him, and to react accordingly.

He knew exactly what this replacement shirt was about, and it had nothing to do with having a crush on him, but was more likely to be because the silly woman had a crush on Daniel Simon, and didn't want to risk losing her job working for him!

He snatched up the receiver as Karen buzzed through to him.

'Good afternoon. Chef Simon. How may I help you?' chanted the cheerful voice on the other end of the line.

Logan tightly gripped the receiver; he was angry at Darcy's actions, but there was no point in losing his temper with someone else over it! 'I would like to speak to Darcy, please,' he answered smoothly, realising that he hadn't even bothered to learn the girl's surname.

'Darcy?' came back the puzzled reply. 'I'm not sure if we have a customer in by that name, sir, but I'll check for you. If you—'

'She isn't a customer, she works there,' he cut in, his resolve to remain polite rapidly evaporating.

'I'm not sure... Just a moment, sir.' The receiver was put down, although Logan could hear a murmur of voices in the background.

Logan drummed his fingers impatiently on his desktop as he waited, a glance at the box containing the silk shirt only succeeding in firing his feelings of annoyance.

'Sorry about that, sir,' the cheerful voice came back on the other end of the line. 'It seems that Darcy will be at the restaurant this evening.'

'At what time?' he rasped.

'We usually arrive about seven o'clock—'

'Book me a table for eight o'clock,' Logan interrupted shortly. 'McKenzie. For one,' he added grimly.

'Certainly, sir. Shall I tell Darcy—?'

'No!' Logan interrupted harshly. 'I—I would like to surprise her,' he bit out through gritted teeth. Surprise wasn't all he would like to do to Darcy!

'Certainly, sir,' the woman accepted. 'That's a table for

this evening, for one, in the name of McKenzie,' she confirmed. 'We look forward to seeing you then,' she added brightly before ringing off.

Logan sat back in his chair, his expression set in grim lines. He very much doubted Darcy would share that sentiment if she were aware he was to be at the restaurant this evening—not when his greatest urge was to wring her slender neck for her!

This evening already promised to be a sight more interesting than yesterday's had turned out to be!

In fact, as he showered and dressed at his apartment later that evening in preparation of leaving for the restaurant, he actually found himself humming tunelessly to himself as he tied his bow-tie.

Because he was going to see Darcy again? he questioned himself incredulously.

Hardly, he admitted ruefully—not unless you counted—

He turned as the telephone on the bedside table began to ring. It was already seven-thirty, and if he was going to make the restaurant for eight o'clock he should be leaving in the next few minutes. But instead of the caller ringing off when he didn't answer, the telephone just kept on ringing. Persistent, or what?

Logan grabbed up the receiver. 'Yes?' he rasped his impatience.

'And a good evening to you too, cuz,' Fergus returned.

'Where are you?' Logan demanded. 'I have some contracts I need you to look at. You're never around when I—'

'Logan, as you are well aware, I am no longer a full-time lawyer. I only continue to act for the family as a favour to all of you,' Fergus cut in smoothly. 'Grandfather needed me in Scotland to discuss a few things with me. But I'm back in London now, so—'

'What sort of things?' Logan questioned warily; his grandfather had a habit of changing his will every month or so, depending on who was in favour at the time. Not that this bothered Logan on a personal level; he was wealthy enough not to be concerned with the McDonald millions. But his mother, as one of old Hugh's three daughters, was likely to be furious if she was cut out of the will yet again. Which meant Logan was sure to get dragged into the situation!

'That's what I rang to talk to you about,' Fergus answered evenly.

'I'm just on my way out, Fergus,' Logan told his cousin after a glance at his wrist-watch. 'Can't it wait until tomorrow?'

'It can,' Fergus answered slowly.

'But…?' Logan heard that hesitation in the other man's voice. It *was* that will again!

'But, I really would rather talk to you tonight.' His cousin confirmed there had been a hesitation.

'Okay, Fergus,' Logan sighed wearily, sure this had to be about his grandfather's will. 'I have a table booked at the Chef Simon restaurant for eight o'clock. Meet me there.' He was sure there would be no problem setting the table for two instead of one.

'The Chef Simon?' Fergus echoed sharply. 'But —'

'Do you have a problem with that?' Logan prompted, unsure whether or not his cousin was involved with anyone at the moment.

The three cousins, Fergus, Brice, and Logan, had been known as the Three Horrors by their family during their growing-up years in Scotland; the Three Macs when they had all gone off to Oxford University together at eighteen; now, in their mid-thirties, all of them having remained unmarried, they had become known in social circles as the Elusive Three.

But the fact that none of them had married did not preclude female involvement in Fergus's life...

'No, no problem,' Fergus answered thoughtfully. 'In fact, it's probably a good idea. A very good idea.' He was obviously warming to the suggestion. 'I have to change first, but I'll be with you as soon as I can.'

Logan slowly replaced his own receiver, frowning deeply. It would be good to see Fergus on a social level; it happened all too infrequently nowadays. Although in the circumstances, it was also a little inconvenient, he realised belatedly...

Never mind, with any luck he would have a few minutes before Fergus arrived to deal with the situation concerning Darcy and the silk shirt.

His mouth tightened grimly as he thought of the meeting ahead. Time for Darcy's surprise!

'The man on table eleven would like to have a word with you, Darcy,' a slightly breathless Katy informed her as she brought some dirty starter plates into the kitchen for washing.

Darcy looked up from what she was doing. 'Me?' She frowned. 'Are you sure he meant me?'

'Darcy. That's what he said.' Katy shrugged, picking up two plates of prawns nestling in an avocado nest before bustling back out into the main restaurant with them.

Darcy felt a sinking sensation in the pit of her stomach. A customer asking to speak to Darcy. She didn't like the sound of that. Not one little bit!

'Better go and see what he wants,' Daniel Simon advised dryly, busy making a sauce for a steak he also had cooking.

Darcy gave him a scathing glance even as she took off her apron and smoothed the black skirt down over her hips, her cream blouse tucked in neatly at her slender waist. 'Keep the customers happy at all costs, is that it?' she returned with barely veiled sarcasm.

He shrugged. 'Well… I draw the line at you selling your body for profit, but other than that…yes!' he answered teasingly.

Darcy's scowl deepened. 'Very funny!' she retorted. 'Can you manage without me for a few minutes?'

He smiled across at her, blue eyes crinkling with humour. 'I think I can cope,' he drawled. 'And, Darcy…' he called softly as she turned abruptly on her heel and flounced over to the doors that led into the restaurant.

She turned at the door. 'Yes?' she replied tautly, chin raised defiantly.

Things had been very strained between them since his announcement yesterday morning, mainly on Darcy's side, she had to admit. But she didn't intend letting him off the hook with a few teasing remarks. Not this time.

'Smile,' Daniel Simon advised ruefully. 'The customers prefer it!'

She only just managed to hold back her biting retort to that particular remark, instead shooting him another scathing glance before going out the swing doors that led directly into the restaurant.

Her footsteps became halting as she instantly recognised the man seated at table eleven. Logan McKenzie!

She had half guessed, because of the parcel she had sent him earlier today, and from the request to speak to 'Darcy', that it might be him—after all, he didn't know her surname. But actually to see him sitting there, looking ruggedly attractive in his black dinner suit and snowy white evening shirt, briefly took her breath away.

Pull yourself together, Darcy, she instructed herself firmly. He might be one of the handsomest men she had ever set eyes on, but she probably wasn't in the minority in that opinion. Besides, she doubted he had come here just to see her. In fact, as she saw the table he sat at was set for two, she was sure he hadn't!

He was looking out the window as she approached, obviously waiting for his dinner guest to join him. Good; that meant their own conversation could be kept to a minimum.

'Mr McKenzie,' she greeted huskily as she stood beside his table.

He turned sharply at the sound of her voice, those blue eyes narrowed as he looked up at her. 'Darcy,' he greeted smoothly, standing up. 'Join me for a few minutes.' He indicated the chair opposite his at the table. 'Unless you would prefer the embarrassment of my handing back your gift in full view of everyone?' He looked pointedly around the already crowded restaurant, his brows raised mockingly as he glanced down at the box that rested out of general view against the leg of his chair.

Darcy sat. Abruptly. Inelegantly. Oh, not because of his threat to embarrass her. It was the latter part of his statement that stunned her. 'Return it?' she confirmed.

'Return it,' he repeated harshly. 'Just what did you think—? I don't like your hair pulled back like that.' He broke off to frown across at her critically. 'It dulls that bright copper colour to a muddy brown,' he opined disapprovingly.

Darcy gave a ghost of a smile. 'That bright copper colour was the bane of my life as I was growing up. I was called Carrots at school,' she explained at his quizzical expression.

'Kids can be the cruellest creatures in the world,' he agreed. 'I'm sure the male population, at least, has been more appreciative of the colour since you reached adulthood.'

Not that she had noticed!

'Maybe,' she conceded dully. 'Mr McKenzie—'

'Logan,' he corrected sternly. 'You can hardly be so formal with a man you're on intimate enough terms with to present with an expensive silk shirt. In the right size, too,' he observed harshly.

Darcy moistened dry lips. 'I had a little help with that,' she admitted huskily, having looked at her father and assessed that he and Logan were about the same physical build. The size of shirt had been easy after that. It had been finding the right shop to buy the shirt that had proved more difficult.

Logan's gaze was cold. 'I'm not going to ask from where. Or who!' he rasped.

Darcy gave him an uncomprehending look. 'If the shirt is the right size,' she began slowly, 'and it's obviously the right colour, then I don't understand why you want to return it…?'

'You don't understand!' His expression became grimmer than ever. 'Darcy, you cannot go around presenting perfect strangers with pure silk shirts,' he ground out between clenched teeth.

She grinned at that, realising as she did so that it was the first time she had found anything to really smile about for some time.

Logan eyed her suspiciously. 'And just what is so funny?' he grated.

'The fact that you have already informed me that you aren't a perfect stranger!' she reminded, her eyes glowing luminously grey.

'I wish you wouldn't do that,' Logan exclaimed, shaking his head.

She raised puzzled brows. 'Do what?'

'Smile.' He looked at her darkly.

It seemed she couldn't win this evening; Daniel Simon told her to smile, because the customers preferred it. But this customer certainly didn't!

Darcy had no idea why Logan should prefer her not to smile—and wasn't sure she wanted to know, either! 'Chef Simon likes us to be polite and friendly with the customers,' she explained frigidly.

Logan studied her. 'And do you always take into account what Chef Simon likes?'

In truth, she was so angry with him at the moment, she really didn't care what he did or didn't like!

But Logan McKenzie had been kind to her yesterday, more than kind, and she owed him a debt of gratitude for the way he had helped her—as well as a new white silk shirt!

'For instance, do you think he would like the fact that you spent what must have amounted to a week's wages on buying a shirt for a man you've only just met?' Logan persisted, the softness of his voice doing nothing to hide his obvious anger.

She blinked. She hadn't thought about the buying of the shirt in that context at all—and now that she did, it still made no difference to the fact that she had ruined this man's shirt, and, as such, had to replace it. Even if it had cost what amounted to a waitress's weekly wages!

Logan sighed heavily. 'What I'm trying to say, and obviously failing to do so, is that I had no intention of telling Daniel Simon what happened between us yesterday—'

'Nothing happened between the two of us yesterday!' Darcy gasped incredulously, eyes wide. That cuddle had been purely platonic, and she dared him to claim otherwise.

'I meant the fact that your behaviour was a little less than professional—'

'It most certainly was not!' she protested, sitting bolt upright in her chair now, her expression indignant.

'Darcy, will you stop being so obtuse?' Logan came back. 'I'm trying to reassure you that I have no intention of telling your boss that you were upset and crying yesterday. In which case, you had no reason to buy me the shirt. Am I making myself clear now?' he asked her frustratedly.

'As a bell,' Darcy answered. 'You think I bought you the shirt in an effort to persuade you not to tell my boss that I was crying all over one of his private clients yesterday. Is that right?' she mused softly—dangerously...!

'Exactly.' Logan looked relieved that he had finally got through to her.

The arrogance. The damned arrogance—

'Sorry I'm late, Logan.' The man's voice was slightly breathless as he approached the table. 'I had trouble finding a taxi,' he explained as he reached them.

Darcy had glanced up as soon as she'd heard the newcomer speak. She had thought Logan was waiting for a woman to join him, but she had obviously been mistaken. The man who now stood beside their table was most definitely male, tall and dark, physically muscular in his black evening suit and snowy white shirt. Apart from the fact that his eyes were dark coffee-brown, and his dark hair was much longer than Logan's, the two men were enough alike to almost be twins.

Those dark coffee-brown eyes narrowed now as he realised Logan wasn't alone, that speculative gaze moving over her assessingly—and clearly coming to the conclusion that, in the black skirt and cream blouse, her hair tied back primly, with no make-up, she wasn't Logan's usual type at all!

That was because she wasn't with Logan!

'I suppose it should have occurred to me that you weren't here alone, Logan,' the newcomer drawled derisively.

'Oh, but he is.' Darcy stood up quickly. 'At least, he was until you arrived,' she informed the coffee-coloured-eyed man smoothly. 'Now if you two gentlemen will excuse me,' she said politely, 'I'll get back to the kitchen.' Where I obviously belong, she could have added, but didn't.

'Darcy!' Logan had stood up too, his hand moving with rapier speed to grasp her arm. 'We haven't finished our conversation,' he told her as she glanced back at him.

'Oh, I think we have.' Her voice was slightly tinged with bitterness, her gaze cold as she looked pointedly at his hold on her arm. 'You're attracting attention,' she warned him evenly, glancing over to where several of the other diners were staring across at them curiously now, as well as Katy and another of the waitresses serving this evening.

'I don't give a monkey's what I'm doing,' he rasped harshly, not sparing those people so much as a return glance. 'I have not finished talking to you—'

'Would you like me to leave, Logan?' the other man put in carefully. 'We can do this some other time.'

'Shut up, Fergus,' Logan snapped, his eyes locked with Darcy's. 'I—'

'Darcy?' the man, Fergus, suddenly echoed sharply. 'Did you say Darcy?' A sharp look in Darcy's direction accompanied his words.

The look Logan shot him was enough to wither a flower

in full bloom, Darcy decided; the effect on the other man was barely negligible, just a slight raising of dark brows.

'I asked you to stay out of this, Fergus,' Logan grated between gritted teeth. 'Would you just sit down at the table and I'll be back in a moment?' Without waiting to see if the other man complied with his instructions he pulled Darcy off to one side of the room, placing them behind a tall potted plant.

She glanced at the patchy green camouflage before looking up at Logan. 'Why don't you just take the shirt? Then we can both forget about the incident,' she pressed as he would have protested once again.

Logan drew in a hissing breath. 'Maybe because I don't want to for—'

'Everything okay, Darcy?' Chef Simon himself was suddenly standing beside them, his glance moving quizzically over them both. 'Katy seemed to think there was some sort of problem?' he elaborated with light enquiry, his eyes mild as they rested on the other man.

Great. Just great. After two days of feeling absolutely furious with this man, Logan McKenzie came along and put her in a position where she was the one put on the defensive! Which was the last place where she wanted to be at the moment!

'No problem,' Darcy was the one to answer tightly. 'Mr McKenzie was just about to sit down and enjoy his meal. Weren't you?' she added pointedly, giving him a glaring look.

'McKenzie?' Chef Simon echoed abruptly, his gaze sharp on the younger man now. '*Logan* McKenzie?' he prompted softly.

'And if I am?' Logan challenged.

Darcy, for one, had had enough of this. The situation had been ridiculous enough before, now it was becoming farcical, with the two men eyeing each other like contestants in a boxing match, apparently deliberating on who would be the one to strike the first blow!

She sighed heavily. 'Logan, will you just go back to your table and get on with your meal?' Her expression pleaded with him to comply with her request. 'We can talk about…that other situation, some other time,' she concluded soothingly as his eyes narrowed. 'If you really think we must.'

'Come and look at the menu, Logan!' The man Fergus had strolled over to join them too now. 'I don't know about you, but I'm starving!' he added with persuasive cheerfulness.

Logan looked ready to argue the point, but a glance at Darcy's rigidly set features seemed to be enough to make him relent slightly, although he still eyed Chef Simon belligerently, even as he answered Fergus. 'Maybe you're right,' he agreed slowly. 'After all, this is a restaurant,' he couldn't resist saying sardonically.

'One of the best,' Chef Simon answered almost as coolly. 'If you'll excuse us, gentlemen; Darcy and I have some food to prepare.' He took a firm grasp of Darcy's arm and almost frogmarched her back into the kitchen, barely waiting for the doors to swing shut behind them before grasping her other arm just as tightly and turning her to face him, effectively holding her immobile in front of him. 'Now perhaps you wouldn't mind telling me what you think you're doing, getting into cosy little corners with a man like Logan McKenzie?' he demanded forcefully, his teasing mood of earlier having completely disappeared.

Darcy stared up at him, not altogether sure how she should answer that particular question…

CHAPTER THREE

'HERE, have a look at a menu,' Fergus advised his cousin as he thrust one pointedly into Logan's hands. 'And for heaven's sake, sit down,' he instructed, already seated at the table himself. 'Then you can tell me exactly what is going on!'

Logan resumed his own seat, aware that several of the waitresses were still watching him curiously. Well, let them; he was more interested in knowing what sort of conversation was taking place in the kitchen between Darcy and her aged lover!

Because he was sure now that was what the other couple were; there was a familiarity between the two that was unmistakable, and a protectiveness emanating from Daniel Simon that Logan couldn't mistake as being anything other than a proprietorial claim.

He had to admit, he had been temporarily stunned by the realisation a few minutes ago, which was the reason Fergus had had to actually instruct him to sit down! He had thought Darcy's infatuation to be a one-sided thing, a crush on an older man, but now he realised there was much more to it than that.

And he didn't like it!

Which also shook him. He'd only met Darcy yesterday but even so, he felt a certain protectiveness towards her himself. The reasons for which he did not want to probe too deeply!

'I mistakenly believed you were on top of this situation

when you told me you were coming to Chef Simon this evening—'

Logan became aware that Fergus was talking to him. 'What did you say?' he asked tersely, his thoughts, if nothing else, still across the room in the kitchen.

Fergus sighed impatiently, putting down the menu. 'Let's have some drinks,' he advised as the wine waiter hovered near their table, obviously waiting to take some sort of order from them. 'I feel in need of one!' he added before turning to the young man and ordering a bottle of Chablis.

Logan pulled his divided thoughts back together, aware that he had no idea what Fergus had been saying to him a few minutes ago. Fergus's rapier-sharp brain was such that inattentiveness around him was not a good idea. During his earlier years as a practising lawyer, the prosecution had lost a lot of cases when coming up against Fergus's defence, for that very reason!

Besides, there didn't seem to be any shouting coming from the kitchen, and Darcy hadn't stormed out, so he could only assume the lovers were kissing and making up. Distasteful as that idea might be to him!

'You were saying...?' he prompted Fergus smoothly, once their wine had been poured and their food order taken; Logan thought he had ordered a fish starter and a steak main course, but he couldn't be sure!

Dark brown eyes studied him over the top of the glass as Fergus slowly sipped his wine. 'Exactly what are you doing here, Logan?' he finally asked thoughtfully.

'At the moment I'm drinking wine.' He held up his glass. 'And shortly, I hope, I shall be eating a meal. Isn't that what one usually does when one comes to a restaurant?' he parried dryly.

'Very funny.' Fergus smiled without humour. 'Might I

ask exactly what is your interest in Darcy?' Brown eyes narrowed speculatively.

'You might ask,' Logan gave an abrupt inclination of his head.

'Well?' Fergus pushed further.

Logan took his time answering, sipping his wine appreciatively, all the time his gaze remaining locked with his cousin's. 'What makes you think there is one?' he finally answered evasively.

Fergus's mouth twisted. 'She was sitting at the table with you when I arrived, the two of you were obviously deep in conversation about something.' He shrugged broad shoulders. 'I don't think that is the behaviour of complete strangers.'

'Or even perfect ones,' Logan returned dryly, lifting up a dismissive hand as Fergus seemed about to snap a reply at what he perceived as Logan's facetiousness.

Maybe it was, but the remark had reminded him too much of his conversations with Darcy for him not to have made that connection...

'She works for the outside catering company of Chef Simon,' he answered his cousin economically. 'We met yesterday when she catered for a luncheon at my office.'

'That's all there is to it?' Fergus pressed.

'Yes, that's all there is to it!' Logan echoed impatiently. 'But even if it weren't—since when have you been my keeper, Fergus?' he charged.

Fergus seemed about to bite out a reply himself, but then thought better of it, drawing in a controlling breath instead. 'When did you last see Aunt Meg? Your mother,' he added softly.

Logan's mouth quirked. 'I know who she is, Fergus,' he replied caustically.

'Well?'

He sighed. 'Fergus, I am not someone standing in the witness box suffering your own particular brand of cross-questioning!'

'I don't do that for a living any more, Logan, and you know it,' his cousin dismissed.

'Then you're giving a good impression of it,' Logan barked.

'I can assure you, I have my reasons for asking,' Fergus returned calmly. 'Have you seen anything of Aunt Meg during the last three weeks or so?'

Logan shifted impatiently. 'My mother is in her mid-fifties, and I am in my mid-thirties; neither of us feels the need to report back to the other on a regular basis!'

'Logan, I'm not criticising your actions as regards your mother—'

'I should hope not,' he rasped, eyes narrowed. 'Because if you were I would feel compelled to ask when you last saw Aunt Cate. Your own mother,' he added pointedly.

Fergus was prevented from answering immediately as the waitress arrived with their starters.

The fish Logan thought he had ordered turned out to be Chef Simon's pâté!

He was losing it, he decided, if he couldn't even remember what food he had ordered. And all because of a young girl who reminded him of one of the deer on his grandfather's estate; extremely nervy, they had glossy red coats and huge limpid eyes, too.

'Do you want to get to the point, Fergus?' he asked his cousin more amiably after tasting the pâté and finding it was delicious.

'The point is, you haven't spoken to your mother recently?' Fergus also seemed more relaxed after tasting the deep-fried Brie that was his own starter.

Logan shrugged. 'Not for several weeks, no,' he confirmed.

'Then your being here this evening is just a coincidence?' His cousin grimaced.

'I've already said so, haven't—? What do you mean, coincidence?' Logan said. 'What does my mother have to do with Chef Simon?' He felt sure he wasn't going to like the answer to that particular question!

Fergus drew in a deep breath. 'Well, as you know, I've been to see Grandfather— Oh, no!' he groaned, glancing towards the door. 'That's all we need!'

Logan had turned too, aware that something momentous seemed to be taking place at the entrance to the restaurant. A short silence amongst the other diners was quickly replaced by the babble of excited voices as they easily recognised the woman who had just swept into the room.

The actress, Margaret Fraser.

At the very same moment, Logan easily recognised the woman who had just entered the restaurant, and also became aware of Darcy finally bursting out of the kitchen—perhaps he had been premature in his assumption the couple in the kitchen were kissing and making up…? Her eyes were glittering with unshed tears, her face was fiery-red—whether from anger or those unshed tears, he wasn't sure.

Darcy glanced to neither left nor right as she strode purposefully towards the doorway, although she stopped in her tracks as she too recognised the woman standing there looking so regally beautiful.

'You!' Darcy burst out with audible disgust, grey eyes definitely gleaming with anger now. 'Well, I hope you're satisfied,' she continued. 'You have what you want; he's all yours!' And with that she continued on her relentless way out of the restaurant, the door slamming behind her.

Logan turned dazedly to Fergus. 'What on earth—?'

'Go after Darcy, Logan,' his cousin told him economically.

'But—'

'For once in your life, will you just do what you're asked without argument, Logan?' Fergus told him sternly, standing up. 'While you do that, I'll try and deal with the situation here,' he offered grimly, looking pointedly across the room to where Margaret Fraser was continuing her entrance into the room.

Although the older woman had obviously been initially shaken by Darcy's verbal attack, she had quickly recovered her equilibrium, smiling graciously at the other diners as she strolled confidently through the restaurant, the three friends she had arrived with trailing behind her.

Of the two prospects, that of following Darcy, or coming face to face with the volatile actress, Logan had to admit he preferred going after Darcy; he would just also prefer to have a clue what was going on before he did so!

'Logan—darling!'

He cringed as, having finally spotted him standing at the back of the restaurant, Margaret Fraser swept across the room to envelop him in one of her theatrical greetings, her perfume overwhelming as she kissed him on both cheeks.

'And Fergus, too,' she recognised warmly, bestowing a similar greeting on him.

Logan watched her dispassionately as she kissed Fergus. Delicately tiny, her shoulder-length hair gleaming like ebony, her hourglass figure shown to perfection in a little black dress—that Logan knew would have cost a small fortune!—the beauty of her face completely unlined, deep blue eyes fringed by thick dark lashes.

There was no doubt that Margaret Fraser was a stunningly beautiful woman. Or, that she was the last person Logan wished to see here this evening!

'Darcy, Logan,' Fergus reminded him, once he'd surfaced from the actress's embrace.

Margaret Fraser gave them both a quizzical frown. 'Darcy...?' she echoed lightly.

Logan's mouth twisted. 'The young woman who insulted you as you came in,' he reminded her dryly.

'Oh, that Darcy.' She nodded vaguely.

'Will you just go, Logan?' Fergus urged in measured tones.

Gladly, Logan decided, nodding dismissively before striding out of the restaurant in search of Darcy.

It didn't take him too long; she hadn't gone very far. She was leaning against the wall outside, her slender body convulsed by desolate sobs.

After her earlier outburst, Logan had no doubt that Margaret Fraser was somehow involved in the desolation of those tears...!

The question was—how?

How could he? How *could* he! And with that awful woman too.

Oh, there was no doubting Margaret Fraser was beautiful enough. But the woman had been married twice already, had announced engagements to other men as many times. How could he even be thinking of marrying—?

'Darcy...?'

She froze at the sound of Logan's voice behind her. She had been so upset when she'd stormed out of the restaurant that she hadn't even noticed him. She doubted the same could be said for her own dramatic exit!

She quickly wiped the tears from her cheeks before turning to face him. 'Mr McKenzie,' she greeted shakily, unable to meet that piercingly probing gaze.

His mouth quirked humourlessly. 'This doesn't seem to be your night, does it?' he sympathised.

He could have no idea! She had thought the disagreement with him in the restaurant was bad enough, but the conversation in the kitchen that had followed had been even worse. And, then, to come face to face with that woman as she'd stormed out—!

'Here,' Logan encouraged gently, holding out a snowy white handkerchief to her.

She gave a watery smile. 'I've only just returned the last one you lent me,' she reminded self-derisively, making no effort to take the handkerchief.

'Which I've just left in the restaurant,' Logan realised. 'Never mind, my cousin will probably return it to me later,' he mused.

So the other man had been his cousin, Darcy noted, which obviously accounted for that strong resemblance between them.

'Take it, Darcy.' Logan continued to hold the handkerchief out to her. 'Your mascara has run,' he observed.

Darcy took the handkerchief with muttered thanks, mopping self-consciously at her eyes—before she remembered that she wasn't wearing mascara, that she hadn't worn any make-up this evening; the heat in the kitchen tended to make it cake! 'Very funny,' she replied, her smile rueful.

'That's better.' Logan nodded his approval of her half-smile. 'I'm sure—whatever it is—that it can't be that bad...?' He bent his head to smile back at her teasingly.

Darcy's own humour faded. 'Worse!' she said with feeling, giving an involuntary shiver. 'You can have no idea.' She shook her head, her expression bleak.

Logan tilted his head, dark brows raised questioningly. 'Want to talk about it?'

Did she? In one way, definitely no! In another way...it

might be quite nice to share this with someone. But was Logan McKenzie, a man she hardly knew, the right someone...?

Probably not, she acknowledged. But if she didn't talk to someone about this soon, she was going to burst! Besides, she had no intention of returning to the restaurant this evening...

She gave a heavy sigh, coming to a decision. 'Would you like to join me for a cup of coffee?'

'Darcy! This is so sudden.' Logan pretended to reel from the suggestion.

'I said coffee, Logan—er—Mr McKenzie—' She broke off, blushing at her own familiarity with a man who was, after all, a customer of Chef Simon. Although, in the circumstances, the formality of 'Mr McKenzie' did seem slightly ridiculous!

'Logan will do,' he assured her, obviously of the same opinion.

She nodded, her cheeks still feeling hot. 'And I was suggesting we go to a coffee bar, not my home!' she explained defensively.

'Aren't I a little overdressed for a coffee bar?' Logan looked down at his dinner clothes.

Of course he was, Darcy realised belatedly. But going to her home really was out of the question. After the heated accusations that had been made in the kitchen earlier, the last thing she needed was for Daniel Simon to return home and find her there with Logan McKenzie!

'We could always go to my apartment,' Logan suggested, his gaze narrowed, seeming to have read some of the indecision on her face. If not the reason for it!

Go to his apartment...! 'I'm sure you can't really be interested in hearing all this,' she burst out. 'I think it might be better if I just went home and—and slept on the whole thing. My mother always told me that things never look so black in the morning,' she went on with forced brightness, knowing this particular situation was going to get worse, not better.

'And my nanny always told me that a problem shared is a problem halved,' Logan came back dryly.

His nanny, not his mother, Darcy noted. But, then, he obviously came from a wealthy background, the sort where the children were cared for by a nanny. Nevertheless, it was very sad if, as it seemed, Logan had had a closer relationship with his nanny than with his own mother. Darcy's own childhood had been spent being cosseted and loved by a mother who had always been there for her. She had been dead just over a year now, and Darcy still missed her deeply.

'Maybe,' she conceded huskily. 'But my mother also warned me about the danger of going to the home of a man I don't really know.'

'My nanny warned me of the same thing where women are concerned,' Logan drawled, taking a firm hold of her arm, at the same time hailing a passing taxi. 'But I'll risk it if you will!'

For the second time in their acquaintance—despite the fact that she was deeply upset, and that she could see no solution to ending this particular misery—Darcy laughed.

Logan froze in the act of helping her into the back of the waiting taxi. 'I thought I asked you not to do that,' he ground out, his jaw clenched.

Darcy blinked up at him dazedly, shaking her head. 'I don't understand—'

'Never mind,' Logan replied tersely, climbing into the back of the taxi to sit beside her before leaning forward and giving the driver his address.

He really was a complete stranger to her, Darcy decided

during the drive to his apartment, Logan gloweringly silent beside her, one glance at his grimly set features enough to stop any attempt at conversation on her part, either.

What if her mother's warning turned out to be a correct one? What if—?

'Do I look like a man who has to drag young innocents off to his apartment in order to seduce them?' Logan suddenly rasped, turning to look at her with cold blue eyes.

Darcy's own eyes instantly filled with tears. He had seemed so kind earlier, so gentle, and now—

'I'm sorry, Darcy,' he said, turning fully towards her. 'One way or another, this evening has turned out a bit of a shambles for me too. But that's no reason to take it out on you! Forgive me?' he prompted, taking one of her hands in both of his.

To her embarrassment, Darcy found herself trembling at his touch. Of all the times in her life to find herself physically attracted to a man—!

She snatched her hand out of his grasp, instantly hiding it beneath the one that still lay on her lap. Although that did nothing to prevent that tingling sensation, just from Logan McKenzie's touch, from spreading up her arm…!

'Of course,' she dismissed sharply. 'But maybe this wasn't such a good idea. I'm sure I've already taken up enough of your time for one night. After all, it's still early enough for you to salvage something from your evening.'

'Too late, Darcy,' he told her teasingly as the taxi came to a halt outside an apartment building.

Apparently the one in which he lived, Darcy acknowledged slightly dizzily as, having paid the driver, Logan took a firm hold of her arm and steered her inside.

She wasn't unused to luxury, her own home being fairly comfortable, and the homes she visited on business for Chef Simon were often opulent, to say the least. But this apartment building—where Logan lived!—was something else.

The man sitting at the desk leapt to his feet as soon as Logan swept through the double glass doors, rushing over to call the lift after greeting him. Darcy's feet sank into the deep pile of the pale blue carpet as she walked at Logan's side. *Clamped* to his side by his firm hold on her arm!

It didn't surprise her that it was the penthouse apartment the lift whisked them up to—after seeing the reception downstairs, she didn't think anything about Logan's home would surprise her any more.

She was wrong!

Where she had been expecting chrome and leather furniture—ultra-modern decor—she found herself stepping into a sitting-room that, although it was expensively furnished, was clearly designed for Logan McKenzie's comfort and relaxation: a thick brown carpet, deep gold-coloured armchairs, mahogany bookcases along one wall, several small mahogany tables placed about the room, and the most amazing paintings on the walls.

It was to one of the latter Darcy was instantly drawn, picturing a deer grazing in the foreground, and a castle behind in the mist. 'A McAllister,' she breathed in awe-struck recognition of the artist, sure she didn't need to ask whether or not it was an original; she doubted Logan McKenzie would tolerate anything else in his home. 'It's beautiful,' she opined as she turned back to face Logan.

He gave a brief nod of agreement. 'It's of my grandfather's home. Can I get you a drink?' He indicated the array of bottles on a side-table.

Darcy was still reeling from the fact that the mellow-stone castle in the painting, shimmering mysteriously in the mist, actually belonged to this man's grandfather. Exactly what had she got herself into...?

'A small whisky, if you don't mind,' she accepted.

'My grandfather would certainly approve of that; he doesn't believe you can trust a woman who doesn't drink whisky!' Logan gave a slight smile as he poured the liquid into two tumblers, handing Darcy the one with the least in it.

With a name like McKenzie, this man's family must come from Scotland—which no doubt also accounted for Logan's grandfather's opinion about women and whisky!

Which was a pity—because normally Darcy couldn't stand the stuff; she just felt in need of a restorative at the moment. The whisky certainly was doing that, initially taking her breath away, but then it quickly gave her an inner warmth.

'Let's sit down,' Logan suggested, suiting his actions to his words, watching as Darcy moved to sit in an armchair across the room from his.

Her action was a bit obvious, perhaps, Darcy acknowledged, but the two of them were completely alone here in the privacy of Logan's home, and she doubted that obsequious man downstairs would come running to her aid if she decided to call for help!

'Now do you feel like telling me what all that was about earlier?' Logan ventured.

She took another sip of the whisky at his reminder of earlier. 'That woman!' she exclaimed with returning anger.

'Margaret Fraser?'

'Yes.' Darcy looked up sharply. 'Did you see her?'

Logan raised dark brows. 'One could hardly miss the entrance of an actress of Margaret Fraser's fame,' he drawled dryly. 'But, I have to admit, I have no idea where she fits into the scheme of things.'

Darcy wrapped both hands around her glass of whisky, wishing it were a hot drink now, so that it could warm her outside as well as in. 'She doesn't,' she replied with feeling. 'That's my whole point!'

Logan shook his head, smiling slightly. 'As clear as mud,' he responded.

Darcy gave a deep sigh. 'It's quite simple, really, my— Daniel Simon, Chef Simon—'

'I know who Daniel Simon is, Darcy,' Logan assured her.

'He's going to marry her!'

There, she had said it, actually had acknowledged it out loud. And it was no more acceptable now than it had been yesterday when she had first been told of the engagement.

'Going to marry whom?' Logan prompted, sitting forward in his chair now.

'Margaret Fraser, of course!' Darcy answered disgustedly.

'You can't be serious?' Logan said disbelievingly.

'Exactly what I said when he told me,' she agreed determinedly. 'But it seems that he is.'

'But I— She's—'

'Incredible, isn't it?' Darcy went on, standing up to pace the room. 'He only met her three weeks ago, and yet he's decided he wants to marry her!'

'Three weeks ago...' Logan echoed, looking thoughtful now.

'Ridiculous, isn't it?' Darcy continued. 'How can anyone decide, after only three weeks' acquaintance, that they want to spend the rest of their life with one particular person?'

'I believe it does happen sometimes,' Logan observed distractedly. 'Although I'm a little surprised—Darcy, are you absolutely sure of your facts?' He watched her with narrowed eyes.

'Positive,' she said with feeling. 'Why else do you think she's at the restaurant this evening?'

'The same reason as everyone else—to eat?'

'And that's another thing.' Darcy kept on going. 'The woman barely eats enough to keep a bird alive; a fine advertisement for a chef's wife!'

Logan's mouth twisted. 'I suppose she has to maintain that wonderful figure somehow.'

Darcy gave him another sharp look. 'Don't tell me you find her attractive too?' she said accusingly.

'No,' Logan answered. 'I can honestly say I am probably one of the few men impervious to her charms, physical or otherwise!'

'Good,' Darcy bit out flatly.

Logan stood up to pour himself another shot of whisky, holding up the decanter to Darcy, putting it down again when she shook her head in refusal. 'Tell me, Darcy,' he began gingerly, after sipping at his replenished glass. 'If—and, I have to admit, I still find it incredible to believe!—Daniel Simon *is* going to marry Margaret Fraser, where does that leave you?'

She shuddered. 'Out of there!' she told him with feeling, putting down her empty glass. 'There is no way I'm going to sit back and just accept all this.' She sighed heavily. 'I shall have to move out of the house, of course—'

'You *live* with him?' Logan interrupted harshly.

'Only for the last couple of months or so,' she replied. 'Since I finished uni. It was never intended as a permanent arrangement, just somewhere for me to stay until I take up a permanent post in September.''

Logan frowned. 'But I thought you worked for Chef Simon Catering?'

'Again, only temporarily. I'm actually a trained kinder-garten teacher.' And until yesterday she had been looking forward to starting her first real job, as such. At the moment, everything looked too black to be able to look forward to anything!

Logan paused, then admitted, 'I'm having trouble keeping up with all this…'

Darcy gave him a sympathetic smile. 'The job with Chef Simon is only a holiday job for me,' she explained. 'Oh, don't worry, I trained as a chef first, before I realised I liked working with children rather than feeding adults! I went back to uni to get the suitable qualifications.'

Logan's frown deepened. 'How old are you…?'

'Twenty-five,' she answered, knowing Logan, like many others, had placed her as much younger than that. She was sure as she got older that this was going to be an advantage, but at the moment it was only a hindrance to people actually taking her seriously.

He looked grave. 'Old enough to know better, then. Darcy, I realise this can't be easy for you, but what are you doing still staying around the man if he's told you he's going to marry someone else?'

She blinked her confusion. 'But he isn't married to her yet…'

'And you intend hanging around until he is?' Logan accused angrily, putting down his whisky glass to stride over to where she stood, and grasping her shoulders.

'Of course,' she assured him determinedly. 'The wedding isn't going to be immediately; I may still be able to persuade him to see sense.'

Logan gave a groan. 'Darcy, you're an attractive young lady yourself—'

'I'm not in Margaret Fraser's league,' she countered.

'Oh, damn Margaret Fraser!' Logan snapped.

Her eyes flashed deeply grey. 'My sentiments exactly!'

'Oh, Darcy…!' Logan muttered before his head lowered and his mouth claimed hers.

It was the last thing, the very last thing, Darcy had been expecting, standing acquiescent in his arms, her head starting to spin as the kiss deepened, became more intimate. Her body moulded against the hardness of his as his hands moved restlessly up and down her spine.

Emotions were high, Darcy's earlier anger turning to a passion she hadn't known she possessed, her lips opening beneath his, her hands beneath the material of his jacket, able to feel the warmth of his body through the silk of his shirt.

Her hair was loose about her shoulders now, Logan having removed that hated band that secured it at her nape, his fingers threaded in the silky softness as his lips sipped and tasted hers, hot breaths intermingled.

She had kissed men before, of course she had, but it had never been like this, feeling as if she were melding into Logan, their bodies a perfect match, her soft curves fitting into the hard hollows of his body.

But it came to a sudden end, Logan wrenching his mouth from hers, looking down at her, almost as if he were confused. 'What am I *doing*—? I'm sorry, Darcy.' His arms dropped from her as he ran the fingers of one hand restlessly through his own hair, his shoulders hunched beneath his jacket. 'I didn't mean to do that.' He turned away. 'I brought you here to try and help you, and instead I almost ended up making love to you. I just— The man is old enough to be your father, for goodness' sake!' he burst out as he turned back to face her.

Darcy took in a deep breath, barely able to think, her lips and body still tingling from Logan's kisses. 'What man?' She frowned her puzzlement.

'Daniel Simon,' he said aggressively.

She swallowed hard. 'I—' She tried to think, to remember what had already been said. But after Logan's kisses, she couldn't think straight at all! 'Logan,' she finally managed. 'I don't know—I don't seem to have explained—Logan, Daniel Simon *is* my father.'

Until just over a year ago, when her mother had died after a brief illness, Darcy's father had been happily married to her mother, their relationship a very loving one.

Which was the reason Darcy was so upset at his announcement he intended marrying again, to the flamboyant actress Margaret Fraser of all people, her off-screen affairs seeming to attract more attention than her actual acting career.

Darcy swallowed hard again as she saw Logan was staring at her, unmoving, a nerve pulsing in his tightly clenched jaw, seeming to be lost for words himself now. It wasn't too difficult to guess the reason why: he probably believed her attitude was an extremely selfish one. It probably was, Darcy accepted dully. But she couldn't help the way she felt...

CHAPTER FOUR

HER father…!

Daniel Simon was Darcy's *father*, and not the lover Logan had assumed him to be.

Apparently he had announced his intention to Darcy of marrying Margaret Fraser…

This was news to Logan, although he had an idea this could have been what Fergus had been intending to talk to him about earlier.

'I realise you must find my attitude—selfish.' Darcy began talking self-consciously. 'I just— My mother only died just over a year ago,' she explained in a sad voice. 'They were married for twenty-eight years. Twenty-eight years! We were such a happy family, too. I just don't see how my father can possibly believe himself in love with someone else after so short a time.' She looked across at Logan pleadingly.

Her father.

Every time Darcy said that, Logan gave an inward wince about what he had believed to be her relationship with the chef. It was his own fault for making such an assumption, of course, although, to be fair to himself, Darcy had never told him her surname—and he hadn't asked her for it, either—or addressed Daniel Simon as her father, or called him 'Dad'!

Although, looking back, Logan could see she had never really stated they had any other sort of relationship, either; he had drawn his own conclusions about that. Completely erroneously, as it turned out!

The problem was, how did he now tell Darcy—?

'I think I had better go,' she said suddenly, her gaze not meeting his as he looked across at her. 'I really have taken up enough of your time.'

'Darcy!' He moved to grasp her arm as she would have turned away, turning her slowly back to face him.

'I know I'm being selfish!' Those deep grey eyes were swimming with tears. 'I just—I can't even begin to think of that woman as my stepmother!' she cried emotionally.

Logan pulled her gently into his arms, cradling her against his chest as the tears fell hotly down her cheeks.

He seemed to be making a habit of this! Not that he was complaining, exactly, he just didn't like to see Darcy upset like this. Although, as far as his equilibrium went, it was probably preferable to her smiling at him.

Once again, in the taxi earlier, her smile had almost been his undoing. There was just something about Darcy's smile that took his breath away...

Which was incredible in itself. She was right when she said she wasn't in Margaret Fraser's league when it came to looks. It was like comparing an exotic bird to a garden robin: the actress was flamboyant, completely unmissable, whereas Darcy—unless she smiled!—would be all too easy to overlook in a crowd. Although Logan had no doubts which woman he—and apparently his inner senses too!— preferred.

'I know it's not much consolation at the moment, Darcy—' Logan stroked her back as the tears began to cease '—but I very much doubt that Margaret Fraser will ever be your stepmother!'

Darcy straightened, wiping away the tears. 'My father is adamant that she will.'

Logan shook his head with distaste. 'And I'm just as sure that she won't.'

Grey eyes widened, eyes that were slightly red from crying. 'But how can you be?' Darcy swallowed hard.

He looked serious. 'Believe me, Darcy, I——' He broke off as the intercom buzzed beside the lift.

After the way the evening had been cut short at the restaurant earlier, his visitor was likely to be Fergus—and his cousin was the last person he wanted to see at the moment. Well...probably not the last person, he conceded; Margaret Fraser had to take that honour!

'Shouldn't you answer that?' Darcy prompted as the buzzer sounded a second time, self-consciously wiping away all trace of her recent tears.

'I should,' he acknowledged reluctantly—because it was the last thing he wanted to do.

He needed time, and space, to talk to Darcy, to explain. But with Fergus waiting downstairs, now certainly wasn't that time. Except Fergus, if allowed up here while Darcy was still here, was sure to say something he shouldn't...!

'Darcy, will you have lunch with me tomorrow?' he found himself asking quickly.

She gave him a considering look. 'What for?'

His brows rose impatiently. 'Because I want to have lunch with you!'

'Why?'

'Good grief, woman, just say yes or no!' he barked, annoyed at her delay.

'If you're only inviting me because you feel sorry for me——' she began slowly.

'I don't feel sorry for you,' he bit out tersely. At least...not yet. If Margaret Fraser ever did become her stepmother, then he might have reason to change his mind! 'I just need to talk to you, okay?' he stated firmly, knowing Fergus would be becoming fed up as he waited downstairs, having no doubt that Parker would already have told his cousin that he was at home!

She gave a half-smile. 'Okay.'

'Good,' he said with relief. 'Now I'm going to take you downstairs, put you into a taxi, and I would advise you to go to bed when you get home and have a good night's sleep. As your mother told you, this won't look so black tomorrow.' Especially as Logan intended finding out exactly what was going on and doing something about this situation himself!

Darcy accompanied him into the lift. 'It certainly couldn't look any worse,' she surmised.

Oh, it could, as Logan knew only too well, but not if it was handled correctly. And he intended to see that it was!

Fergus levelled a look of cold criticism at Logan, for keeping him waiting, as Logan stepped out of the lift with Darcy at his side.

'I'll be back in a moment,' Logan told him as Fergus would have spoken, vaguely noting that Fergus did have the parcel from the restaurant with him. He could sort that out with Darcy tomorrow. 'I'm just going to put Darcy into a taxi.' He strode out of the building, Darcy held firmly at his side, before his cousin had a chance to make any sort of reply.

Darcy turned to him before getting into the back of the taxi. 'You really have been very kind,' she said almost shyly.

It wasn't a characteristic too many people would apply to him, Logan thought wryly, but if that was how Darcy saw him, he wasn't about to argue with her!

'Lunch tomorrow,' he reminded her economically. 'Twelve-thirty. At Romaine's. It's—'

'I know where it is,' she assured him, reaching out to touch his arm. 'And thank you once again.'

Logan stood and watched the taxi until it disappeared around the corner at the end of the road, his thoughtful expression turning to one of hard determination as he turned to walk back into his apartment building.

'Nice-looking girl,' Fergus remarked as he followed the glowering Logan into the lift.

Logan gave him a cold look. 'She's Daniel Simon's daughter,' he rasped. 'But then you already knew that, didn't you?' he added accusingly as the two men stepped into his apartment, Logan striding straight over to the drinks tray to replenish his glass, taking a grateful sip before pouring another glassful for Fergus.

'Thanks.' Fergus took the glass. 'Yes,' he sighed, bending his long length into one of the armchairs. 'I already knew that. This, apparently, is yours.' He held up the parcel.

'Thanks.' Logan took it and put it on the side without further comment. Fergus didn't have to know everything!

His cousin sipped the whisky. 'I know we were practically brought up on this stuff, but I'm not sure we should be drinking it at the moment; neither of us has eaten much this evening!'

'Come on.' Logan came to a decision. 'I'll cook us both an omelette—and then you can bring me up to date with exactly what is going on!'

It only took a few minutes to prepare the omelettes and a salad to go with them, the two men shortly seated at the breakfast bar; Logan had lived on his own a long time now, was more than capable of feeding himself. And anyone else who happened to be here. On this occasion, it happened to be Fergus.

Except it didn't really just happen to be Fergus...

He gave his cousin a sideways glance. 'Am I right in supposing that your recent visit to Grandfather was because my mother is about to announce her engagement to restaurateur and chef, Daniel Simon?'

His mother.

Margaret Fraser.

Although it was hard to believe—he chose not to believe it himself most of the time!—the actress Margaret Fraser was his mother. She was also Fergus's Aunt Meg.

With that cascade of dark hair, beautiful unlined face, youthfully slender body, Logan knew his mother didn't look much older than himself. But she was, undeniably, his mother. He knew—because he had lived with the unpalatable fact long enough!

He had been dumbstruck earlier when Darcy had announced her father's intention of marrying the beautiful actress. He and his mother had never been particularly close, but in the past his mother had at least told him—warned him?—when she'd intended either marrying or becoming engaged to someone. This time Logan had been taken completely unawares. Although he knew Darcy, innocent of the true facts, had misunderstood his silence. He intended explaining everything tomorrow when they met for lunch.

'It was,' Fergus confirmed with another sigh. 'Apparently she told him of her plans when she visited him at the weekend.'

'And, because the two of us have always been close, you were chosen to break the news to me,' Logan guessed.

His cousin shrugged. 'Ordinarily Aunt Meg would have told you herself. But in this case there seems to be a—complication.'

'Darcy,' Logan confirmed knowingly.

'Darcy,' Fergus confirmed flatly. 'Apparently she isn't too keen on Aunt Meg marrying into the family.'

'I wouldn't be too keen on having her marry into my family, either!' Logan exclaimed.

Fergus turned to give him a considering look. 'You know I've never tried to interfere in your relationship with Aunt Meg—'

'Then don't start now,' Logan warned him softly.

'I have no intention of doing so,' his cousin assured him calmly.

Logan gave him a sceptical glance. 'No?'

'No,' Fergus confirmed lightly, sipping the white wine Logan had opened to accompany their snack meal. 'Firstly, because there's no point; your feelings on that issue are your own business. Secondly,' he continued as Logan would have spoken, 'because I believe there is something of much more urgency for us to discuss.'

Logan raised dark brows. 'Such as?'

'Such as how you're going to break it to Darcy that you're Margaret Fraser's son? Without her hating your guts when you've finished, I mean,' Fergus added.

He had been wondering the same thing himself!

'I am right in surmising Darcy doesn't have a clue about that, aren't I?' Fergus mused.

'Maybe if you hadn't arrived here so precipitously—'

'Don't try and blame this situation on me.' Fergus held up defensive hands.

Fergus was right; Logan knew that he was. He should have told Darcy the truth the moment she'd mentioned Margaret Fraser. But, if he had, he also knew that Darcy would have looked at him with the same dislike she had looked at his mother. And that wasn't something he wanted from Darcy. He wasn't sure what he wanted from her, but it certainly wasn't for her to lump him in with the same antipathy she felt towards his mother.

He had less than twenty-four hours to think of a way of

telling Darcy the truth—without the end result being, as
Fergus had pointed out only too graphically, her hating his
guts!

She was late.

She knew she was late. Almost fifteen minutes, to be
exact. With any luck Logan would have tired of waiting
for her to arrive and already have left! After the morning
she had had, she didn't feel up to this meeting, too!

She had taken Logan's advice the evening before, going
to bed shortly after getting in, amazingly falling asleep too,
not even waking when her father had returned home at his
usual one o'clock in the morning. She had been exhausted,
of course, from all the emotional trauma of the last few
days.

Not that she'd felt any better when she'd woken at nine
o'clock this morning, knowing by the sound of the radio
downstairs that her father had already been up. Margaret
Fraser was sure to have told him of her own parting shot
as she'd left the restaurant the evening before.

She had been right about that; her father was absolutely
furious that Darcy had caused a scene in the restaurant of
all places. Her reply, that scenes were what Margaret
Fraser enjoyed the most, had not gone down too well, and
the argument that had followed had been far from pretty.
With the end result that Darcy had told her father exactly
what he could do with his holiday job, and that she would
be looking for a flat of her own later today.

Darcy still cringed when she thought of that argument;
until the last couple of days she could never remember
being at odds with her father about anything. As far as she
was concerned, it was all Margaret Fraser's fault!

But it was partly because of that argument with her father that she had been late changing into her figure-fitting

navy-blue dress in readiness for joining Logan for lunch. Partly...

Logan hadn't left the restaurant!

She could easily see him as she entered the room, sitting at a window table. Very much as he had done last night. Except a lot had happened since she'd spoken to him at Chef Simon yesterday evening!

Logan was looking as arrogantly handsome as ever in a grey suit, and—unless she was mistaken—the white silk shirt she had sent to him yesterday...

He stood up as she was shown to the table, Darcy noting several female heads turning in their direction as he did so. No doubt those women had been wondering—as she had last night—who would be joining this attractive man for lunch; she doubted any of them had expected him to be interested in a mousy little thing like her!

Ordinarily they would be right...

'Darcy!' Logan greeted warmly now, indicating for the wine waiter to pour her some of the white wine he had obviously ordered while he'd waited for her to arrive. 'Unless you have to work this afternoon?' He quirked dark brows across the table at Darcy.

'I am, at the moment, what I believe is known in acting circles as "resting",' Darcy answered brittlely.

Logan gave her a sharp look. 'I wouldn't know,' he said dismissively.

'Neither does my father,' she scorned. 'But I have a feeling, when he marries Margaret Fraser, that he will very quickly find out!'

'Shouldn't that be *if* he marries her?' Logan replied hardly.

'Not according to my father,' Darcy muttered with remembered bitterness.

'Presumably, by your earlier remark, you're no longer working for him?' Logan queried.

'We've decided that a parting of the ways—in all areas of our lives—is probably for the best. Nice shirt,' she added dryly, looking at the snowy white garment.

'Damn the shirt,' Logan came back. 'No, I didn't mean that the way it sounded,' he continued a little less fiercely. 'It's a beautiful shirt. And I don't think I ever thanked you for it,' he admitted awkwardly.

Perhaps he wasn't a man who was used to accepting presents. Probably more used to giving them, Darcy decided.

'You're welcome.' She nodded. 'What made you change your mind about keeping it?' she enquired as she picked up the menu and began looking down the food on offer.

'The fact that you had obviously gone to a lot of trouble to get it for me,' he said quietly.

'I see.'

'Darcy—'

'Have you tried the lasagne here?' She looked over the top of the menu at him. 'I believe it's supposed to be delicious.'

'Darcy, I'm trying to talk to you,' Logan said wearily.

She raised auburn brows. 'I thought you invited me out to lunch?'

'I did,' he returned sharply. 'Because we need to talk.'

'And not eat,' she replied understandingly, closing her menu and putting it down on the table-top. 'Talk away,' she invited.

Logan paused. 'You seem different today somehow,' he said eventually.

'Do I?' she returned in that same brittle voice. 'Perhaps we should put that down to the fact that I'm a little—upset, that my father and I are no longer even speaking to each other because of his decision to marry a woman I can't even begin to like!'

Her voice broke slightly over the last. To her inner annoyance. She was rather tired of appearing immature and emotional in front of this man. In fact, she was more than tired of it!

'It will all sort itself out, Darcy,' Logan told her gently, reaching out to put his hand over one of hers.

She looked across at him with cool grey eyes. 'You seem very sure of that?'

'I am.'

'How can you be?'

His hand squeezed hers slightly. 'Because I—'

'May I take your order now, sir? Madam?' The waiter stood expectantly beside their table.

'No, you—' Logan broke off his angry retort, drawing in a deep, controlling breath, before turning to Darcy. 'Are you ready to order?'

She smiled up at the waiter to make up for Logan's previous terseness. 'Lasagne and a green salad, please,' she ordered—but wasn't absolutely sure she would be around long enough to eat it!

'I'll have the same,' Logan announced.

'Would you like any water with your meal—?'

'No, we wouldn't,' Logan interrupted the man gratingly, glaring up at him with icy blue eyes.

'Thank you.' Darcy smiled up at the young man again, receiving a grateful grin in return before he left in the direction of the kitchen.

Logan removed his hand abruptly from covering hers. 'I realise that until a few hours ago you were a waitress yourself,' he said harshly. 'But do you have to be so friendly with the staff?'

Hurt flared in her eyes at the unwarranted rebuke, making them appear almost silver. 'Good manners cost you nothing, Logan,' she returned briskly. 'Besides, why should I ruin his day, just because mine isn't turning out to be so brilliant?'

'Thanks,' Logan said sarcastically.

Darcy sighed. Why was she even bothering to go through with this? Because she was still angry? Or because she wanted to see just how far Logan was willing to go in this charade? The latter, probably, she acknowledged heavily. But this whole situation was grating on her already frayed emotions.

'Logan, exactly what is it you want from me?' she demanded suddenly, giving up all pretence now of this being a pleasant lunch together. Not that it had ever been that in the first place—on either side!

Logan looked startled by the question, eyeing her warily. 'What do you mean?'

She pursed her lips, her expression scathing. 'Stop treating me like an idiot, Logan,' she bit out disgustedly. 'I mean, what do you, Margaret Fraser's son, want from me?' she challenged, her eyes gleaming silver once again.

She hadn't been able to believe it this morning when, in the heat of their argument, her father had told her exactly who and what Logan McKenzie was, demanding to know what the two of them were plotting together.

At the time, she had even been too numbed by her father's revelation to defend herself properly against those accusations…

Logan McKenzie was the son of that—that woman?

Incredible as it seemed to her, it appeared that was exactly what he was. The actress looked barely in her thirties herself, and yet she had a son aged in his mid-thirties. And her son was Logan McKenzie…

Darcy had thought him so understanding yesterday evening. Hey, she had even thanked him for being so kind to her!

He had kissed her too. Worse, she had kissed him back...!

But she now realised Logan had had his own reasons for being so nice to her, and those reasons involved his mother!

She felt so stupid now when she thought of all she had said to him, all the things she had confided in him.

But most of all, she was angry. Furiously so. Which was the reason she had decided to continue with the arrangement of meeting Logan for lunch today; she wanted the pleasure of telling him to his face exactly what she thought of him!

'Well?' she challenged again at his continued silence, her expression mutinous.

He drew in a ragged breath. 'I'm not sure I know what to say...' he finally admitted.

Darcy bridled. 'An apology might not be amiss! What on earth you hoped to achieve by not telling me the truth from the beginning, I have no idea, but I can assure you that whatever it was you have failed miserably; nothing you could do or say would ever convince me to accept your mother marrying my father!'

She was breathing hard in her agitation, more angry with Logan McKenzie now than she was with her father. At least her father had been honest with her.

Logan frowned darkly. 'Let me assure you, Darcy,' he began, 'I am no more enamoured by the idea of the two of them marrying than you are. Until you told me about their plans, I had no idea it was even a possibility!'

She didn't believe him. He had to be fighting his mother's corner. Besides, if what he claimed were really the case, once he'd become aware of the engagement, aware of her own aversion to the relationship, he had had plenty of opportunity to tell her the truth about his own relationship to Margaret Fraser. If he had wanted to. Which he obviously hadn't.

Although, she did remember he had assured her that he didn't believe any marriage between the older couple would ever take place…

'My father, a mere restaurant owner, isn't good enough for your mother, is that it?' she retorted as the idea suddenly occurred to her, remembering that painting on the wall in Logan's apartment of the castle that was the Scottish family home. The home where Margaret Fraser had probably been brought up.

Logan waved the waiter away impatiently as the young man would have brought their meals to the table. 'Darcy—'

'That is it, isn't it?' she accused incredulously as the idea began to take hold. 'Exactly who do you think you are? More to the point, who do you think your mother is? Because from where I'm standing, she's nothing more than a—'

'Darcy!' Logan's voice was icily cold now, his expression glacial. 'There's nothing you could say about my mother that I haven't already said or thought of her myself. But that doesn't mean I'm willing to sit quietly by while someone else is rude and insulting about her!'

Darcy glared at him. 'In that case, you must spend most of your life getting into fights or arguing with people; I haven't met a single person yet with a nice thing to say about your mother!'

Logan's mouth twisted. 'Except your father, of course.'

'He's just besotted,' she defended. 'Knocked off his feet by the glamour that surrounds her.' She shook her head.

'I just hope he comes to his senses before he does something stupid—like marrying her!'

'Oh, he will,' Logan said grimly.

Darcy's eyes gleamed angrily. 'Because you intend seeing that he does,' she guessed. 'I don't know which one of you I despise more—you or your mother!'

Logan's throat moved convulsively. Whether from anger or some other emotion, Darcy couldn't tell. And she didn't particularly care, either.

'I've had enough of this.' She threw her unused napkin on the table before bending down to pick up her bag. 'Enjoy your meal, Logan—both portions of it!' She stood up to leave.

Logan's hand snaked out and grasped her painfully around the wrist as she would have walked away, looking up at her with darkened blue eyes. 'Darcy, I'm on your side—'

'I don't have a side, Logan,' she assured him contemptuously. 'Thanks to you and your mother, I don't even have a home any more, either!' Her voice broke slightly as she realised the truth of her words.

She mustn't cry. She would not give Logan the satisfaction of seeing her cry again. As far as she was concerned she never wanted to set eyes on Logan, or his mother, ever again!

'Let me go, Logan,' she ordered coldly, looking down to where his fingers encircled the slenderness of her wrist.

'And if I don't?' he challenged softly.

Her eyes returned slowly to the harsh arrogance of his face, her chin rising defiantly. 'Then I'll be forced to kick you in the shin,' she told him with determination.

Darcy watched as some of the harshness left his face, to be replaced by what looked to her suspiciously like amusement. No doubt at what he considered to be the childishness of her claim, she realised.

It was the spur Darcy needed to carry out her threat, lifting her leg back before kicking forward with all the impotent rage that burned inside her, the pointed toe of her shoe making painful contact with Logan's shin bone.

She knew it was painful—because of the way Logan cried out in surprise at the agony shooting up his leg!

But it had the desired effect; he let go of her wrist, to move his hand instinctively to his hurting shin.

'Goodbye, Logan,' Darcy told him with a pert smile of satisfaction, before turning on her heel and walking out through the restaurant, totally unconcerned with the curious looks that were being directed towards her, the confrontation not having passed unnoticed. Which wasn't surprising, when Logan had actually yelled out his pain!

Her feelings of defiant satisfaction lasted until she got outside. They even lasted while she flagged down a taxi and got inside. It was only when the driver asked her where she wanted to go that her feelings of self-satisfied anger deflated.

Because, as of this morning, when she had told her father she was moving out of their home, she had nowhere *to* go...

CHAPTER FIVE

'SHE hates my guts!' Logan informed Fergus, his cousin having arrived at his office a few minutes ago. Logan hadn't returned from the restaurant very long ago himself.

Fergus stayed perfectly relaxed as he sat opposite Logan. 'I see you handled the situation with your usual tact and diplomacy,' he drawled mockingly.

Logan scowled as he remembered Darcy's earlier fury. In truth, he hadn't had a chance to be either tactful or diplomatic—how could he have been when Darcy had already been well aware of exactly who he was when she'd joined him for lunch?

He had thought he'd had time to tell her the truth himself, but it should have occurred to him that her father, or someone else, might just drop that little bit of information into a conversation before the two of them had met today! No wonder Darcy had seemed different when she'd arrived at the restaurant!

He glowered across at Fergus. 'I didn't get a chance to handle anything—her father must have already told her I was Margaret Fraser's son!'

'Poor Logan.' Fergus grinned, shaking his head.

'You don't know the half of it,' he retorted.

'No—but I'm hoping you'll tell me,' his cousin returned expectantly.

Because Logan needed to talk to someone, because, for once, he wasn't sure what to do next, where Darcy was concerned—or if, indeed, he should do anything!—he told Fergus exactly what had transpired at the restaurant earlier.

'And then she kicked me!' he concluded slightly in-credulously several minutes later.

Incredulous—because he hadn't really thought she would carry out her threat. One thing he had definitely learned from this third meeting with Darcy—never under-estimate her!

Logan was so lost in thought that for a couple of minutes he didn't even notice the twitching of Fergus's mouth, his cousin's Herculean effort not to actually laugh. A fight he finally lost, bursting into loud laughter. At Logan's expense.

'She really kicked you?' Fergus sobered enough to choke out. 'In the middle of the restaurant?'

'Actually it was in the middle of my shin,' Logan re-plied succinctly. 'And, yes, she kicked me; I have the bruise to prove it!' Once out of the restaurant, sitting alone in the back of the taxi, he had had a chance to look at his leg; a purple bruise was already forming there.

'Can I have a lo— No, perhaps not,' Fergus amended as he saw Logan's mutinous look. 'I think I like the sound of your Darcy,' he murmured appreciatively.

'She isn't *my* Darcy,' Logan rasped, not even sure she would ever talk to him ever again.

Which was a pity. He could still remember how good she had felt in his arms when he'd kissed her the evening before—

Forget it, Logan, he instructed himself sternly. There were too many complications attached to being attracted to Darcy Simon. Complications he intended dealing with at the earliest opportunity.

'So what happens now?' Fergus seemed to guess at least some of his thoughts.

Logan pondered awhile. 'A meeting with my mother,' he bit out with obvious reluctance.

His cousin looked surprised. 'Will that do any good?'

'Probably not,' Logan conceded. 'But it might make me feel better. These are good people she's playing around with.' He paused, then went on, 'Daniel Simon was recently widowed; he doesn't need someone like my mother messing up his life.'

'Hmm.' Fergus looked thoughtful. 'I wonder—' He broke off as the door opened after the briefest of knocks.

Talk of the devil—!

Logan's gaze narrowed as his mother walked unannounced into the room, as beautiful as ever in a fitted black suit and vibrant red blouse.

'Karen told me you were closeted in here with Fergus,' she said, closing the door behind her.

Fergus had stood up at his aunt's entrance, glancing across frowningly at Logan's set expression as he made no effort to do likewise. 'I was just on my way to see Brice.' He moved to kiss Logan's mother lightly on the cheek. 'Bye, Aunt Meg. Logan,' he added evenly.

Logan ignored the warning note in his cousin's voice; he had no intention of pulling any verbal punches where his mother was concerned.

'Do stop scowling, Logan,' his mother snapped impatiently once they were alone, a frown marring the creaminess of her brow. 'I know I don't usually call on you here, but I've come to ask you for advice—'

'Ask me for advice?' he said incredulously; this wasn't what he had been expecting at all.

Not that he had expected to see his mother here in the first place; if the two of them ever did meet, it was usually by accident and not design. As in the restaurant yesterday evening...

She gave him an irritated look as she sat down in the chair Fergus had so recently vacated, crossing one shapely knee over the other. 'You seem to be on friendly terms with Darcy—'

'Correction, Mother, I *was* on friendly terms with Darcy,' Logan cut in coldly, having physical evidence to prove that friendship was a thing of the past! 'Before she realised I was your son. Or do I mean before she realised you were my mother? Same thing, I suppose,' he ruminated. 'The end result is that Darcy no longer sees me as a friend.' Or anything else. And it was amazing how much more that pained him than the bruise on his leg!

'I see,' his mother said. 'What am I going to do, Logan?' She gave a confused sigh.

Logan couldn't hide his surprise. This was something new; his mother had never asked for his opinion—on anything!—before...

'About what?' he prompted harshly.

'Darcy, of course,' she returned. 'Do try not to be obtuse, Logan,' she admonished. 'I'm sure you are well aware by now of my engagement to Daniel Simon. Darcy's father.'

'I believe someone did mention it to me, yes,' he drawled.

His mother's eyes flashed deeply blue, two wings of angry colour in her cheeks. 'If you ever showed an interest in me or my life, Logan, then I would have told you myself! But as you don't...' She drew in a ragged breath.

'Last night you gave the impression you had no idea who Darcy was,' Logan said questioningly.

'Well, of course the two of us have never met, but I guessed who she was last night,' his mother retorted. 'I was merely trying to avoid a scene in the restaurant. You see, Darcy doesn't like the idea of her father marrying me—'

'I wonder why.' He couldn't resist his taunting reply.

His mother gave him a considering look. 'You know, Logan, you were a lovely little boy, so loving and caring. What happened to change that?'

Logan could see, by the genuine puzzlement on her face, that she really wanted to know. Incredible!

'Life, Mother,' he bit out economically. 'Yours,' he added hardly as she would have spoken.

She shook her head. 'I can't believe that after all these years—Logan, I know I've made mistakes in the past—'

'Mistakes!' Now he did stand up, moving impatiently to the coffee machine that stood on a sidetable, pouring himself a cup of the dark steaming brew. 'Your life has had all the stability of a helter-skelter! And during the early years, after my father died, when I wasn't old enough to have a say in things, you took me along for the ride!' he concluded disgustedly.

His mother's eyes, as she looked up at him, flooded with sudden tears, and she suddenly looked very tiny, and slightly vulnerable. Strange, he had never seen her in quite that light before...

No! His mother was a consummate actress—she had made a living the last thirty years, both on and off screen, with that acting! He must not be taken in and manipulated by the role she apparently saw herself in now.

'I know I was far from the perfect mother to you, Logan, after your father died,' she began huskily. 'But I just missed him so much—'

'I missed him too,' Logan told her coldly.

'I know,' she acknowledged shakily. 'I do know, Logan,' she insisted as he would have protested. 'But it isn't the same. I had lost the man I loved. *I* was lost, seemed to lose all direction in my life. I—I made a mistake when I married again, I know that,' she admitted. 'But I was lonely, and— There's nothing I can do or say now that will take away the past. It's the future we have to look to now.'

Logan looked down at her. This really was a different role for her. His mother had never spoken to him in this way before, never confided in him in this way. And he wasn't quite sure how to deal with it.

'Whose future are we talking about, Mother?' he queried. 'Yours or mine?'

She looked back up at him, her gaze unwavering. 'I love Daniel Simon,' she told him quietly. 'He's the first and only man I have loved since I lost your father. And I would like to marry him.'

Logan shrugged. 'The last I heard, that's exactly what you intend doing!'

She shook her head. 'Not without Darcy's approval.'

His mouth quirked. 'Again, the last I heard—and she didn't exactly use these words, you understand?—there was about as much chance of Darcy giving her blessing to her father marrying you as there is of hell freezing over!'

'I know,' his mother agreed dully.

Logan gave her a probing look, still unsure of her in this mood. Usually his mother gave the impression she was totally in control of her world, and the people in it. Perhaps that was the trouble this time…?

'Dear, dear, Mother, don't tell me that you aren't more than capable of talking Daniel Simon round to your way of thinking?' he taunted. Goodness knew there were very few men who could resist his mother's brand of charm!

'You just don't understand, do you, Logan?' His mother shook her head sadly as she returned his gaze unblinkingly. 'Daniel is all for going ahead with the marriage, and dealing with Darcy's feelings later; I'm the one who won't go ahead with the wedding without his daughter's approval.

It's no way to begin our married life together, and I will not come between father and daughter.'

Now Logan was really puzzled. Could it be, could it really be, that his mother really did love Daniel Simon, that she was putting someone else's happiness above her own...? It would be the first time!

His mother gave a shy smile at his obviously stunned expression. 'Not exactly the way you see me, is it, Logan?' she ventured ruefully. 'Maybe if we had been closer the last twenty years or so—'

'As you are well aware, Mother, I despised Malcolm Slater, the man you chose to marry after my father died, preferred to live with Grandfather rather than with you and him,' he revealed with distaste.

'I despised Malcolm myself by the time we were divorced,' she admitted.

Logan was surprised. 'You did?'

His mother gave a wistful smile. 'I did. Mainly because I lost my son during the five years we were married. Logan, why do you think I feel so strongly about having Darcy's approval to her father marrying me? It's because I know how it feels to lose your child in those circumstances,' she continued firmly. 'I lost you for that very reason, because of the way you felt about Malcolm,' she said emotionally. 'And although it may be too late to do anything to salvage our own relationship, I won't do that to Daniel and Darcy!'

Logan stared at his mother, wondering, just wondering, if he could have been wrong about her all these years...

She looked at him with unwavering blue eyes. 'I need your help, Logan. I need you to help me persuade Darcy that I really do love her father, that I intend making him happy. Will you help me?'

Would he?

Wasn't his mother, a woman he had kept at an emotional distance for more years than he cared to think about, asking him to take on the role Darcy had already cast him in at lunch-time—that of championing his mother?

Did he really want to champion his mother? Could he believe the things she was saying to him?

More to the point, didn't Darcy already hate him enough…?

'Call for you, Darcy,' her grandmother called up the stairs.

A call for her…?

Who from? Apart from her father, no one else knew she had been staying with her maternal grandmother the last couple of days; and her father only knew because her grandmother had thought she ought to tell him.

Again, it was only a temporary arrangement, Darcy having found an apartment to rent that very afternoon. Unfortunately the current tenant wasn't moving out until next week.

She ran down the stairs to pick up the receiver in the hallway. 'Yes?' she prompted warily.

'Darcy,' Logan McKenzie greeted with satisfaction. 'You're a very difficult young lady to track down.'

Darcy had stiffened as soon a she'd recognised his voice, her hand tightly gripping the receiver. 'Why did you bother?' she returned coldly.

'I thought you might be interested to know that I'm in hospital with a broken shin-bone,' he came back mildly.

'You're what?' she gasped, remembering all too vividly the way she had kicked him on the leg at the restaurant two days ago.

'That got your attention anyway.' He chuckled. 'Actually…' he sobered '…I exaggerated slightly.'

'How slightly?' Darcy ventured warily.

'I'm not in hospital. And my shin-bone isn't broken.'

'In other words, it was a total lie!' Darcy came back disgustedly.

'Fabrication,' he corrected smoothly. 'It isn't nice to call someone a liar, Darcy.'

'Logan,' she sighed wearily, 'what do you want?'

'To have dinner with you this evening,' he returned lightly.

She was taken aback at the unexpected invitation. 'Why?'

'You really are the most suspicious young lady!' he opined dryly. 'Why not?'

The reasons for that were too numerous to go into. And some of them were reasons she couldn't possibly tell Logan! As in, she found him too disturbingly attractive. As in, she dared not run the risk of having him kiss her again. As in—

'Oh, come on, Darcy,' he cajoled at her continued silence. 'It's only dinner.'

Only dinner...

But what were the implications behind the invitation? What was it supposed to achieve? Because she had no doubts that under ordinary circumstances—such as his mother not being about to marry her father!—Logan would never have thought of asking her out to dinner! He must already be aware, she had no influence with her father whatsoever!

'Logan, my father is a grown man, an adult, perfectly capable of making his own choices and decisions without any help from me,' she told him decisively.

'Yes?'

'Yes!'

Was he being deliberately difficult? Didn't he realise

how much it hurt her to be at odds with her father like this?

Apart from picking up her things from the house, telling her father where she was staying for the moment, the two of them hadn't spoken to each other for two days. And this man's mother was responsible for the estrangement between the two of them.

'I don't see what your problem is, Darcy,' Logan told her. 'You've got what you wanted, by fair means or foul, so why—?'

'What do you mean?' she cut in.

'My mother has broken off her engagement to your father,' Logan revealed.

'She's done what?' she gasped, suddenly feeling light-headed, so much so that she sat down abruptly on the chair beside the telephone.

'Yes, it's all off,' Logan told her happily. 'My mother broke the engagement last night.'

'Why?' Darcy breathed dazedly.

'Does it matter?' Logan replied. 'It's what you wanted, isn't it?'

She hadn't wanted her father to marry Margaret Fraser, no, but until she knew the reasons for the broken engagement she could feel no satisfaction in its ending. If the couple had simply decided they had made a mistake after all, that was okay, but if it were for any other reason— such as her own objections to it!—then it wasn't okay at all. If Margaret Fraser had been the one to break the engagement, how must her father feel now?

'I must say,' Logan continued at her silence, 'I expected you to be happier about it than this.'

But how could she be—when she knew her father must be totally miserable?

This was awful. A mess. It was a mess *she* had helped create…!

'Then you thought wrong, Logan,' she responded. 'And if you think I'm going out with you this evening to celebrate—'

'I think celebration is far too strong a description of my invitation,' he returned mildly. 'Admittedly, we can no longer drink a toast to the happy couple, but—'

'How can you be so unfeeling?' she interrupted accusingly. 'I have no idea how your mother feels, but my father is probably devastated, and all you can do is—'

'Now just a minute, Darcy,' he put in impatiently. 'You're the one that wanted an end to this engagement, and now that you have it, you—'

'You wanted it as much as I did,' she defended heatedly. 'You were the one who thought my father wasn't good enough for your mother!'

'I don't think I ever said that—'

'But you thought it!' Darcy persisted. 'And now it seems, no doubt with more than a little help from you, that your mother is of the same opinion. How dare you presume—?'

'Stop right there, Darcy,' Logan told her firmly.

'I most certainly will not,' she retorted angrily. 'You made it perfectly obvious that you were not happy about my father marrying your mother—'

'As obvious as you did that you weren't happy about my mother marrying your father. Now we've both got our wish, so what are you complaining about? You've won, Darcy,' he taunted. 'Defeated the dragon. In fact, she's turned tail and run!'

Except Darcy didn't feel as if she had won anything— she felt terrible! Not that she had changed her opinion about the older woman's unsuitability for her father, she had just realised—with blinding clarity!—that she didn't have the right to decide those things for another person, least of all her father.

'I think you're an unfeeling brute,' she told Logan indignantly.

'Because I won't pretend to be upset about all this?' he scorned.

'Because you're a selfish swine!' she returned forcefully.

'Does that mean you won't be having dinner with me this evening?' he queried wryly.

'Not this evening, or ever!' she cried. 'Now, if you'll excuse me, I have to go out.'

'To see your father?'

'Mind your own damned business!' she shouted, before slamming down the telephone receiver.

He was a brute. An unfeeling swine. Didn't he care that his mother was probably as unhappy at the broken engagement as her father no doubt was? Obviously not. He was just glad his mother's engagement to—in his eyes!—a totally unsuitable man was at an end.

Well, they would see about that!

CHAPTER SIX

LOGAN felt like a murderer returning to the scene of the crime!

Not that Chef Simon, with its warm decor, wonderful smells of cooking food, and efficiently friendly staff, was anything like a scene of carnage and destruction. Logan just felt, as he walked through the restaurant doorway, as if he were entering an arena!

Although, admittedly, it was an arena of his own making!

He had no doubt that Darcy really did hate his guts after their telephone conversation earlier. But he had been the way that he had for a reason.

Except he hadn't been able to resist coming here this evening, if only to see if Darcy had been reunited with her father. Which had, after all—although she would never see it that way—been the purpose of his telephone call to her earlier...

'Good evening, Mr McKenzie,' the *maître d;* greeted him warmly. 'How nice to see you again.'

Coming here to eat twice in one week probably did seem a little excessive, Logan accepted, but his curiosity, he inwardly admitted, had got the better of him.

'James,' he said with a nod, after reading the name on the man's lapel. 'My secretary telephoned earlier and booked a table for me. For one,' he added dryly; this eating alone was becoming a habit!

'She certainly did,' the *maître d'* assured him. 'The same table as before, if that's okay with you?'

Why not? He was no more in the mood for company this evening than he had been three days ago!

'Fine.' He smiled. 'And I'll endeavour to get through the whole evening this time, too,' he quipped.

The other man waved away his words of apology. 'Your cousin explained that you had been called away unexpectedly.'

Thank you, Fergus, Logan thought to himself.

'Is Darcy—Miss Simon in this evening?' he casually asked the *maître d'* once he was seated, a menu placed in front of him.

For a brief moment, the other man's cheerful efficiency deserted him, but it was quickly brought under control, although his smile, when it came, still seemed to Logan to be slightly strained. 'She certainly is, Mr McKenzie,' he confirmed. 'Would you like me to tell her—?'

'No! Er—no,' Logan repeated less harshly. 'I merely wondered if she was here tonight, that's all. Thank you,' he added dismissively.

Darcy was here! Hopefully, everything was all right with her world again.

'Can I get you something to drink, Mr McKenzie?' the *maître d'* offered politely.

'Whisky,' he accepted tersely.

'Water and ice?'

Why didn't the man just go away and leave him alone? Logan complained inwardly.

Because now that he was here, seated at this table, he had realised his tactical error!

He could have telephoned and ascertained whether or not Darcy was here this evening; he hadn't had to subject himself to eating here alone…! To eating here at all!

Not that the food wasn't excellent; he just had to get through the whole evening now, with Darcy only feet away in the kitchen, knowing that she wouldn't even give him the time of day if she knew he was in the restaurant. It was not a feeling Logan was familiar with. In the past, he had always been the one to sever any relationship with a woman he had been involved with.

Except he hadn't been involved with Darcy. Not in that sense, anyway...

So what was he doing here? Damned if he knew!

'No water or ice,' he answered the *maître d'*.

This time Logan made sure he knew exactly what he was ordering: a fish starter, and a steak main course!

He had no doubts, when it arrived, that it was delicious too; he just didn't taste a mouthful of it! So conscious was he of Darcy working in the kitchen only a short distance away, that every time the kitchen door swung open he couldn't stop himself casting a furtive glance in that direction.

This was ridiculous!

Why should he feel so uncomfortable? He hadn't done anything other than tell Darcy what was, after all, the truth. Besides, if she was back working here, she had obviously made amends with her father. She should be thanking him!

Except Logan knew that she wasn't, that she thought him an unfeeling, selfish brute. Or words to that effect. Why was it, he wondered ruefully, that the person in the middle of a situation, once things had calmed down slightly, always ended up as the target for both sides? Because his mother was no more enamoured of him at the moment than Darcy obviously was. She—

'What are you doing here?'

So intent had he been on his own thoughts—the penalty for eating alone?—that Logan hadn't even noticed that Darcy had actually come out of the kitchen, that she had been moving from table to table chatting politely with the diners.

Until, that is, she had obviously spotted him sitting alone at the window table!

Logan placed his knife and fork down on his plate before looking up at her. 'It isn't quite what I had in mind when I invited you out to dinner, but it will have to do,' he admitted.

She was wearing the restaurant uniform of a cream blouse, teamed with a black skirt, her hair once more secured at her nape, her face flushed from her exertions in the kitchen.

Or was it anger at seeing him here?

Probably, he acknowledged self-derisively. Well, if she was surprised to see him here, he had been thrown a little himself by having her suddenly appearing beside his table in this way!

'I hope you aren't about to make another scene in your father's restaurant, Darcy,' he taunted mockingly at her continued silence. 'Two in one week just isn't on, you know,' he went on. 'People will start coming here for the "cabaret" rather than the food if that's the case!' He looked up at her with assessing blue eyes.

She drew in a sharp breath, seeming to be having difficulty keeping her temper in check.

But obviously also knowing Logan was right about her not making a scene...!

'No, I'm not about to make a scene,' she finally replied. 'I merely asked what you're doing here,' she repeated in measured tones—although her eyes told a different story, flashing that dangerous silver colour.

'I would imagine the same as everyone else,' he said casually, looking about them pointedly to the tables full of chattering diners. 'Eating!'

Her hands clenched at her sides. 'But why here?' she demanded. 'Or did you simply come to gloat?'

'Smile, Darcy,' he advised softly. 'People are beginning to stare.'

'Let them,' she dismissed hardly. 'Contrary to what you and my father both seem to think, I am not a Cheshire cat who smiles on demand!'

Logan looked at her consideringly. 'I would have said, with that copper-coloured hair, that you resemble a fox rather than a cat—Cheshire, or any other kind!'

'Logan—'

'Well, that's promising, at least,' he drawled. 'I was expecting you to call me something much worse than my first name,' he explained as she frowned questioningly.

And it was promising. After the way their telephoned conversation had ended earlier, he had winced at some of the things she might say to him when—or if—they ever met again. Logan was pretty okay in those circumstances!

'Do you have a few minutes?' he requested mildly. 'I thought you might like to join me for a glass of wine,' he explained as her sceptical expression deepened.

'Join you—!' She looked ready to explode, bringing her temper back under control with effort. 'Logan,' she finally said evenly, 'if I pick up a glass of wine I am more likely to tip the contents over your head than I am to drink it!'

This was more like the Darcy he knew and— And what? Logan had no idea what. But he did know his evening had suddenly taken on a sparkle, the very air about them seeming to zing with life. One thing he had found about Darcy: she had never bored him.

Which was extraordinary in itself, because in all of his relationships with women so far, intimate or otherwise, he had invariably found himself bored within a few meetings...

'That would be a waste of a good Borolo.' He picked up his glass and toasted her with it before taking a sip of wine. 'This really is an excellent wine—are you sure you wouldn't like to join me for a glass?' He quirked dark brows.

'Absolutely positive,' Darcy assured him between clenched teeth. 'I have to get back to the kitchen. Thanks to you, and your mother, I am absolutely rushed off my feet this evening!' she muttered grimly.

'Well, I can see that the restaurant is busy,' he murmured with a glance round at the full tables. 'But surely that's what you want, isn't it? I don't see how my mother or I are involved?'

'Really?' The sarcasm unmistakable in her tone, Darcy pulled out a chair to sit opposite him at the table. 'Then I'll explain shall I?' She leaned forward, silver gaze steady on his face. 'You obviously advised your mother that she was making a mistake in marrying my father—'

'I—'

'If you will kindly let me finish?' Darcy carefully enunciated each word.

Perhaps he had better; she looked ready to explode. Teasing apart, he really didn't advise another scene in the restaurant so soon after the last one!

'Thank you,' she accepted scathingly at his nod of agreement. 'On your advice, your mother broke her engagement to my father. My father, in the meantime, has decided that he needs a complete break away from everything. Your mother. Me. The restaurant. Everything,' she repeated emotionally. 'And so—'

'Are you telling me that your father isn't in the kitchen?' Logan cut in softly.

'That's exactly what I'm telling you.' Darcy nodded firmly.

'Then who—?' Logan shook his head, his gaze narrowed. 'Are you also saying you're the one that has been producing all the meals this evening?'

She seemed to bristle at his tone, sitting up straighter in her chair. 'Was there something wrong with your meal?'

'No, not in the least,' he assured her a little amazedly.

In fact, the food had been excellent. He just hadn't realised that Darcy could cook like that, thought when she'd said she helped her father out in the kitchen that she probably peeled the vegetables or something. Although perhaps—he dared a glance at Darcy's set features!—he hadn't better actually say that...

The fact that Daniel Simon wasn't actually in the kitchen this evening also explained the *maître d*'s behaviour earlier. Clearly, although James and the rest of the staff were doing their best to make it appear otherwise—and succeeding too, Logan allowed—all was not right in the Chef Simon kitchen this evening!

'I did tell you I had trained as a cook,' Darcy reminded him stiltedly.

Yes, she had, but he had still thought— 'You're very good,' he complimented. 'I had no idea it wasn't your father in the kitchen producing this mouth-watering food.' His scallops had been wonderful, his steak succulent enough to melt in his mouth.

'That's probably because he helped train me,' she explained tersely.

'He did a good job,' Logan said distractedly. 'But where is he now?'

Darcy sat back, eyes having suddenly darkened to smoky grey, her mouth trembling slightly as she spoke. 'I have no idea,' she told him shakily. 'He didn't tell me. And I didn't like to ask.'

Logan stared at her. Twice he opened his mouth to

speak. And twice he closed it again, without having uttered a word.

Another thing that was unusual about Darcy—she had the power to render him speechless!

Why didn't Logan say something? Anything!

The shock of seeing Logan in the restaurant this evening had quickly been superseded by a desire to tell him— again!—exactly what she thought of him, and what he had done to her family, such as it was. Well, she had done that. Only to have Logan simply stare across at her with those enigmatic blue eyes.

This had been the most awful day. That earlier telephone conversation with Logan. Going to see her father. Only to have him tell her that he just had to get away for a few days, and would she take over the cooking at the restaurant while he was away. In the circumstances, what else could she have said to the latter but yes?

Although she had tried to talk to her father about the situation, sure that going away at this time would solve nothing. But he'd remained adamant that was what he was going to do, and nothing Darcy could say would persuade him otherwise.

And so she had agreed, in his absence, to take over the restaurant. But that didn't mean she was at all happy about this situation.

Or the part Logan McKenzie had played in it!

'Well, why don't you say something?' she finally snapped, the tension becoming unbearable.

Logan grimaced. 'I'm not sure I know what to say.'

'That must be a first!' she scorned.

He looked at her reprovingly. 'Insulting me isn't going to help this situation, Darcy,' he admonished.

'Perhaps not—but it makes me feel better!' she told him forcefully.

'I don't doubt that. But it isn't going to bring your father back. From wherever it is he's gone to lick his wounds.'

'Wounds that your mother inflicted on him!' Darcy accused defensively, her cheeks flushed fiery-red now. 'She's the first woman he's really looked at since my mother died, and she's just thrown his love back in his face as if it meant nothing to her!'

Logan gave her a considering look. 'Shouldn't you have thought of that before you threw your ultimatum at him?'

'I didn't—'

'Giving up your job with him here, moving out of the family home, isn't issuing him with an ultimatum: her or me?' Logan reasoned softly.

The flush in her cheeks faded until they were deathly white, her eyes, a dark smoky grey, the only colour left in her face. 'I merely—merely—' She broke off, her bottom lip trembling so badly she couldn't speak any more. 'If you'll excuse me,' she muttered, before getting up and making her way blindly back to the kitchen, relieved when she heard the door swing shut behind her, tears falling hotly down her cheeks now, waving away the concerned gestures of the other staff working in the kitchen.

But she didn't feel quite so relieved when she felt strong arms move about her, pulling her in to the hardness of what she easily recognised as Logan's chest. He had followed her!

'This is becoming too much of a habit,' he said ruefully a few seconds later as a white handkerchief appeared in front of her face.

Darcy took the handkerchief, her sobs subsiding as she mopped up the tears.

She had tried all evening not to think about her father,

and the reason he had gone away, but when Logan had spoken of it just now she had known he was right. Her father hadn't just gone away to escape from his heartbreak at his broken engagement, he had gone away to get away from her too!

And she had taken the easy option and turned her anger at herself round on Logan...

Okay, so he wasn't exactly in favour of the marriage, either, but Darcy doubted very much that he was in a position to order his mother to break her engagement to Darcy's father. No, Margaret Fraser had made that decision all on her own. Much as she hated to admit it, Darcy's aversion to the marriage might just have had something to do with that decision...

'Darcy—Oops!' One of the waitresses stood awkwardly just inside the kitchen, grimacing slightly as she saw Darcy in Logan's arms, and the way the kitchen staff studiously avoided looking at them. 'I'm sorry for interrupting,' the girl said uncomfortably. 'Table number ten liked your creamed spinach so much they wondered if they could have some more,' she explained.

Logan glared across the room at the poor girl. 'Tell table number ten that—'

'No, it's all right, Logan,' Darcy interrupted his angry reply, pulling out of his arms to turn and smile at the waitress. 'Give me a couple of minutes, okay?' she encouraged before turning back to Logan. 'I really do have to get on with this now. I—'

'I'll go back and finish my meal,' Logan told her. 'Then I'll wait and take you home afterwards,' he stated determinedly.

She had to admit, she didn't exactly relish returning to her father's empty house, having moved back there earlier this evening, deciding it would be fairer to her grandmother, now that she was to take over at the restaurant, if she wasn't arriving back at all hours of the day and night. But the alternative of having Logan accompany her home wasn't exactly appealing either!

'This isn't a subject for negotiation, Darcy,' he told her firmly as he obviously saw the doubt in her expression. 'We still have things we need to talk about.'

She hadn't intended negotiating; she had been going to say a very firm no thank you to his suggestion. But one look at his determinedly set features and she knew she would be wasting her time. And time wasn't something she had to waste this evening!

She nodded. 'I should be finished here by about twelve-thirty.'

'Fine,' he accepted briskly before turning on his heel and returning to the main restaurant.

Darcy drew in a deep breath before turning to smile at the four members of staff who helped out in the kitchen each evening. 'The show's over, folks,' she told them. 'And we have a restaurant to run,' she added.

But she couldn't exactly say her mind was on what she was doing for the rest of the evening, conscious of the fact that Logan was waiting to take her home. Her concentration wasn't helped by the fact that, at eleven o'clock, Logan, his meal obviously over, came through to the kitchen, making himself comfortable on a stool at the back of the room.

Everyone else working in the kitchen had already gone home for the evening by this time, Darcy just dealing with late desserts, doing most of the clearing away herself too.

Logan didn't say a word, but Darcy was conscious the whole time of his brooding presence at the back of the room.

'I shouldn't be much longer,' she told him awkwardly,

just after midnight, the last customers gone from the restaurant now, most of the staff too, just the night's takings to deal with.

'Take your time,' he said. 'I'm not going anywhere.'

Except back to her home with her! To talk, he'd said. But what else did they have to say to each other? She was coming to accept they weren't exactly on different sides in this situation—but they certainly weren't on the same side, either!

Much as she wished she didn't, she still remembered the way he had kissed her three days ago.

More to the point, she remembered the way she had kissed him, too!

CHAPTER SEVEN

LOGAN remained deliberately silent during the drive to Darcy's home, appreciating the fact that she was tired from her hectic evening's work. He also didn't like the fact that she looked so exhausted. In fact, he felt more than a little angry towards her father for leaving her in the lurch in this way. It was his restaurant; he had no right just going off like this and leaving everything to Darcy!

'Can I get you a coffee?' she offered once they had reached her home, switching on the lights as she led the way to the kitchen at the back of the house.

'No, you can't,' Logan answered decisively. 'You can sit there—' he suited his actions to his words, gently pushing her down into one of the pine kitchen chairs that stood around the table. '—while I make you a cup of coffee. You've waited on people enough already this evening,' he told her as he began to search through the cupboards for the makings of the coffee. 'I had no idea there was so much hard work involved in running a restaurant,' he admitted, as he put the kettle on to boil.

Darcy gave a strained smile. 'Normally there would be two chefs in the kitchen each evening, but it was David's—the other chef night off, and—'

'With your father's disappearing trick, you were left to carry the whole load,' Logan finished for her.

'Actually, I was going to say—and I didn't feel it was fair to David to ask him to come in and do an extra evening,' Darcy corrected.

'I don't think it fair of your father to just go away and

93

leave everything to you like this, either,' Logan told her crossly. 'It's a broken engagement, not the end of the world!' He placed a steaming coffee in front of Darcy before sitting down at the table himself to sip at his own cup.

She looked across at him consideringly for several long seconds. 'Have you ever been in love, Logan?'

He sat back, unable to hide his surprise at the intimacy of her question. No one had ever asked him a question as personal as this before, not even Fergus and Brice, and goodness knew, they were as close to him as two brothers!

'Have you?' he finally came back defensively.

Darcy smiled, a less tired smile this time, the respite from the pressures of cooking, and the warming coffee, obviously reviving her slightly. 'Once,' she said. 'But I don't think it counts.'

Logan didn't agree. What sort of man had she once been in love with? Had he loved her in return? And if so, where was he now?

'I was nine,' Darcy told him with a mischievous smile. 'And he was ten.'

She really was starting to feel better if she could tease him in this way, Logan accepted wryly.

But he wasn't; why had it bothered him so much when he'd thought Darcy had been in love with someone else...?

'An older man,' he returned dryly to cover his own confusion.

'Hmm.' She smiled, sipping her coffee. 'But I don't think it's a legitimate basis from which to judge how my father must be feeling at the moment,' she added with a pained grimace.

She might be right; as Logan had never been in love—even at the age of nine or ten!—he really couldn't say.

Although he was still of the opinion that his mother was no great loss to Daniel Simon's life!

He had listened to what his mother had had to say two days ago, and perhaps he even understood her a little better now, but too much had happened, too much time had passed, for him to be able to trust completely the things she had said to him.

Logan shrugged. 'I'm sure he'll get over it,' he said.

Darcy gave him a troubled look. 'I wish I had your confidence. Perhaps if I spoke to your mother—'

'Whatever for?' he burst in incredulously, putting down his coffee-cup. 'The other evening you couldn't even bear to be in the same restaurant as her!'

Darcy pulled a face. 'But maybe I was wrong about her. I've been giving all of this a lot of thought—with my father the way that he is, I thought I had better! And if *he* loves her—'

'You said yourself that he didn't, that he couldn't know how he felt about her after only three weeks of knowing her,' Logan reminded her. He had known his mother for thirty-five years—and even he wasn't sure that he loved her!

Margaret was his mother, yes, and as such he knew he should respect and protect her, but love...? He wasn't sure.

Darcy gave a heavy sigh. 'I thought this broken engagement was what I wanted, but now that it's happened— I just can't bear to see my father so unhappy!'

'Better a brief unhappiness now than a lifetime of it,' Logan assured her.

Darcy tilted her head to one side as she gave him another of those considering looks. 'You really never have been in love, have you?' she stated evenly.

'I simply doubt that it's a basis from which to build a lifetime relationship,' he dismissed hardly.

Darcy gave a start of incredulity. 'What other basis is there?' she gasped.

'I have no idea—I've yet to see a successful relationship!' Logan claimed scornfully.

His mother said her marriage to his father had been happy, but Logan had been too young himself when his father had died to be able to judge the truth of that statement. And Margaret's second marriage had been like a battlefield.

No, he had decided long ago, if he ever took the drastic step himself of getting married—and he couldn't conceive of a situation where he ever might!—then it most certainly wouldn't be because he believed himself in love with a woman. Love made you vulnerable, left you completely exposed to the whims and fancies of the other person. It was not a feeling Logan ever wanted to experience for himself!

A cloud marred Darcy's creamy brow. 'I find that very sad.'

And she did look sad. So much so that Logan found he didn't like being the cause of that sadness. 'Hey,' he chided teasingly. 'We aren't here to discuss how I see love and marriage. It's your father you're concerned about, remember?'

Not the right thing to say, Logan decided as he saw her sadness deepen. But she had been getting too close, asking him questions he would rather not answer.

'I really would like to talk to your mother,' she decided firmly. 'Do you think it could be arranged?' She looked at him with clear grey eyes.

Not by him it couldn't! His mother was definitely not someone he would like Darcy to meet.

'For what purpose?' he probed guardedly.

Darcy looked perplexed. 'To be honest, I have no idea.

It's strange, but somehow I feel the fact that we both love my father gives us a bond of some kind... Can you understand that?' She looked at him questioningly.

Maybe. But— 'Have you forgotten that my mother has broken her engagement to your father?' he reminded her. 'Hardly the act of a woman in love!'

'But that's the whole point. I need to know *why* she broke their engagement,' Darcy persisted, 'If it had anything to do with me—'

'Even if it did, what can you do about it?' Logan insisted, still not sure himself that he believed his mother when she said she wouldn't marry Daniel Simon, the man she professed to love, if it meant damaging his relationship with his daughter. Because if he believed that, he had to believe her regret concerning their own relationship too. And he wasn't sure he could do that... 'My mother is a woman not easily swayed by the needs and wants of others.' He replied.

Logan didn't like the way Darcy was looking at him now, knowing he must have given away too much of his own resentment and bitterness towards his mother.

But after Margaret Fraser had rung him this morning to inform him she had ended her relationship with Daniel Simon, Logan's one thought had been to let Darcy know it was over, too. Darcy had responded predictably by going straight to her father. Daniel Simon was the one who had altered the scenario by going away in the manner that he had. Now Darcy, after expressing deep loathing for his mother, was asking to meet her. Logan wasn't sure he would ever understand women... Correction—most women, he had found, were all too easy to understand; it was his mother and Darcy who were enigmas!

Darcy continued to look at him determinedly. 'Will you

introduce me to your mother, or do I have to find some other way of meeting her?'

'Why can't you just accept that it's over?' Logan demanded. 'And be grateful that it is!'

'Will you?' she persisted stubbornly, totally ignoring his words.

He stood up abruptly. 'No, I will not!' he roared. 'Why can't you just leave the situation alone? My mother will carry on acting, your father will get over his disappointment, and you—'

'*I* won't rest until I've talked to your mother!' Her eyes flashed up at him.

Logan stared down at her frustratedly for several long seconds. She really was the most stubborn—

As stubborn as he was himself...?

Probably, he acknowledged ruefully, his anger starting to fade. If Darcy really was serious about meeting his mother—and it appeared she definitely was!—then wouldn't it be better if he were present when the two met?

Most definitely!

'Okay,' he conceded frustratedly. 'I'll speak to my mother some time tomorrow and see if she's willing to meet you. Will that satisfy you?' It was as far as he was willing to go, so it had better suit her!

Darcy's answer to that was to smile.

At which point Logan felt that sledgehammer hitting his chest, again totally taking his breath away!

'Thank you, Logan,' Darcy said with warm gratitude before standing up. 'Can I get you some more coffee?' she offered politely.

'Coffee...?' he echoed in what sounded like a strangulated voice.

She turned from filling the kettle, brows arched. 'Unless you have to leave now?'

Normally she was very tired when she returned from working in the restaurant, but tonight she was too hyped after the evening's activities to be able to go straight to bed, and would need a couple of cups of coffee and a short read before feeling she would be able to sleep. But obviously Logan hadn't had the same stimulus.

He did look rather grim, however. No doubt because of her determination to meet his mother. But she couldn't help that, felt it was something she needed to do.

Although, in the last few minutes, she had had to do some revising of her earlier opinions concerning Logan's relationship with his mother. She had assumed Logan didn't want her father to marry his mother because he wasn't good enough for her. Logan's comments since arriving back here implied something else completely; he didn't like his mother. Which to Darcy was awful. How could he not like his own mother? And if Logan didn't like her, what chance did *she* have of doing so...?

'Logan?' she prompted worriedly as he still made no effort to answer her. Just stared at her with those dark blue eyes...

He stepped forward, standing only inches away from her now. 'What the hell is it about you?' he muttered angrily.

Darcy gave him a startled look. 'What?'

Logan shook his head self-disgustedly. 'Every time you smile I want to kiss you.'

Her eyes widened even more, and she was too stunned by the admission to step back as he pulled her effortlessly into his arms, anything she might have wanted to say dying in her throat as Logan's mouth claimed hers.

He might feel an urge to kiss her every time she smiled, but every time he did she melted! Her legs became like jelly, the soft contours of her body melded into his much harder ones, her lips parting invitingly as the kiss deepened.

Her hands moved up to grasp the width of his shoulders. Not that she was in danger of falling; Logan was holding her much too tightly against him for that to happen. She just liked the feel of Logan, the hard strength of his body, the caress of his hands against her.

Hands that moved restlessly across her back, and lower spine, before searching out the soft pertness of her breasts, Darcy gasping low in her throat as he sought and found the hardened tips, the caress of his thumbs sending pleasure coursing through her whole body.

Logan broke the kiss, his lips against her throat now, tongue seeking the hollows at its base as he moved aside the material of her blouse, his breath warm against her breasts.

Darcy was burning, yearning, wanted—she wanted this never to stop!

Logan's lips and tongue touched the creamy softness of her breasts, his hands trembling slightly as they moved to unbutton the front of her blouse, peeling the garment aside once he had done so, the clasp of her bra easily dispensed with too.

There was a slight flush in Logan's cheeks as he looked down at her nakedness. 'You are so beautiful!' he groaned achingly, his hands cupping her breasts as his lips moved down to kiss each rosy tip, his tongue moving moistly against the aching hardness.

Darcy felt weak with desire, her body hot and feverish, trembling so badly now she could barely stand up. She wanted this man. Wanted him naked against her, wanted to feel the hard planes of his body, to caress him as he was her.

But the first feel of her fingers moving against his shirt buttons seemed to break the spell for Logan, one of his hands moving to clasp both of hers even as he moved slightly away from her.

Darcy looked up at him, her eyes dark with passion, questioning why he had stopped her.

'This is not a good idea,' he grated, moving sharply away from her, bending to pick up her blouse, not even looking at her as he held the garment out to her.

Darcy grabbed the blouse, consternation washing over her in embarrassed waves.

What was she *doing*?

With her acquiescence, it had taken Logan exactly—she glanced at the clock on the wall—ten minutes—to have half her clothes off.

What on earth must he think of her? A couple of hours ago she had been hurling verbal abuse at him, and yet just now—just now—Oh, dear!

'I think I had better go.' Logan spoke, his expression weary as he ran a hand through the thick darkness of his hair. 'I—I'm sorry, Darcy,' he added tersely.

He was sorry?

Darcy wasn't sure she would ever be able to look him in the face again! Logan had kissed her as she had never been kissed before, caressed her as she had never been caressed before, touched her as she had never been touched before. He had seen her semi-naked, for goodness' sake!

'I really am sorry, Darcy,' he repeated heavily.

Her blouse was back on, the buttons firmly fastened. After that first glance at the grimness of his expression, Darcy found she couldn't look at him, found herself looking anywhere but at Logan.

'Maybe you should just go,' she suggested, staring unseeingly at the tiled floor.

'Yes.'

But he didn't move. Even though she wasn't looking at him, Darcy could still feel his presence in the kitchen, knew that he hadn't gone.

'Please, Logan!' she finally pleaded, not sure how much longer she could remain standing on her feet.

'Yes,' he repeated evenly. 'I—I'll call you tomorrow. Concerning the meeting with my mother,' he explained as Darcy looked up at him in query.

'Of course,' she realised flatly, turning away again. For a moment she had thought he meant something else!

That he wanted to see her again. That the two of them might be able to—

Fool, she berated herself. She and Logan came from different backgrounds, lived in different worlds, had only been thrown together at all because of her father's relationship with his mother; Logan would never have looked at her twice under normal circumstances.

Although, a little inner voice reminded her, neither of them had known of that connection that time in his office…!

She moistened dry lips. 'It might be better if, in future, I didn't smile at you,' she teased huskily in an effort to lighten the tense atmosphere that now existed between them.

A pretty dismal effort it was too, Darcy acknowledged, but she had to make a start somewhere. After all, this man might—just might, if her father and his mother ever sorted out their differences—one day be her stepbrother. Now there was a sobering thought!

'Yes,' Logan agreed quietly. 'I'll call you as soon as I've spoken to my mother.'

She nodded. 'I shall be at the restaurant from eleven o'clock in the morning, preparing for the lunch-time trade.'

Logan shook his head. 'It really is a hell of a life. At this rate, I'll have to make another booking with the Chef Simon outside catering company just so that I can have a private conversation with you!'

In the circumstances, Darcy thought it was probably better if he didn't; their private conversations had a way of turning into something else completely!

'I'm sure my father won't be away for very long,' she told him noncommittally. 'I'll walk you to the door, shall I?' she added pointedly. She really did need some time alone!

'Let's hope he isn't,' Logan answered her question as they walked out into the hallway. 'You already look exhausted!'

Devastated was probably a more apt description, Darcy acknowledged with a sickening lurch in the pit of her stomach. She was having serious problems coming to terms with what had just happened between the two of them, couldn't quite believe it had happened.

And Logan didn't look much happier!

No doubt he was wondering what on earth had possessed him to kiss her at all, let alone make love to her in the way that he had. Despite what he had said during the heat of their lovemaking, she was not beautiful, and never had been. Although her figure wasn't bad, warm and homely probably best described her looks.

It was her smile that had been his undoing, Logan had claimed in his defence. A claim she had joked about earlier. But in future, all teasing apart, she really would try not to smile at him. Unless she wanted to find herself being well and truly kissed by him!

Logan paused in the open doorway. 'Lock the door behind me when I leave,' he advised. 'I can't say I'm exactly happy at the thought of you alone in this big house all night.'

Well, the obvious alternative wasn't acceptable, either!

'Believe it or not, Logan, and despite what you may have thought to the contrary, because I happen to be staying here with my father at the moment—' she resorted to sarcasm to dispel her feelings of awkwardness '—I've actually been taking care of myself for some time now!'

His gaze was scathing as it moved over her face. 'Then, on the evidence I've seen so far, you aren't doing a very good job at it!' he rasped.

Darcy drew in a sharp breath. 'I'm sure a lot of people are interested in your opinions, Logan—but I don't happen to be one of them!'

'Lock the door anyway, hmm?' was his parting shot before he strode over to unlock his car.

Darcy didn't wait long enough to see him open the car door, let alone start the engine and drive away, slamming the front door behind him, being deliberately noisy as she turned the key in the lock.

She leant weakly back against that closed door. How could she have let that happen? she berated herself with a self-disgusted groan. Not only had Logan kissed her—again!—but he had touched her more intimately than any other man ever had, too.

Every time she thought of those intimacies, Logan's hands and lips on her body, she wanted to crawl into a corner and hide! And she didn't even have the effect of *his* smile to claim in her own defence; Logan rarely smiled, and she didn't think she had seen him laugh once.

Possibly because of that unhappiness she had sensed between him and his mother? She simply didn't know.

Just as she didn't know how on earth she was going to face him again tomorrow, this time possibly in the presence of his mother...!

CHAPTER EIGHT

LOGAN was not looking forward to this meeting. But it
had nothing to do with his mother being there—and everything to do with Darcy's presence!

Logan had done as she'd asked, and telephoned his
mother this morning—at a time he knew she would be up.
After years of working in the theatre, mornings were not
Margaret's best times. Except that he knew she was filming for a television series at the moment, so her hours were
not quite so antisocial; in fact, she sounded quite cheerful
when she took Logan's call.

Logan wished he felt as cheerful. But, after a virtually
sleepless night, he was feeling tired and bad-tempered. He
had laid awake for hours thinking about Darcy Simon, trying to fathom out why it was she affected him in the way
she did. It did not help to improve his temper this morning
that he simply hadn't been able to come up with an answer!

Blaming his reaction on a smile just wouldn't do. For
goodness' sake, it was only a smile!

Darcy was nothing like the women he was usually attracted to: beautiful, self-confident, emotionally indepen-
dent women. Darcy was only beautiful when she smiled—
and that wasn't too often when around him, thank goodness. Her self-confidence could do with a little working on
too. As for her emotional independence—he had lost yet
another handkerchief to her tears!

So why was it that he couldn't get her out of his mind,
that even last night, when he had gone to the restaurant, it

had been in an effort to make sure everything was once again right with her world?

Then to cap it all, he had deliberately set himself up for yet another meeting this week with his mother—for Darcy's sake!

He closed his eyes momentarily. A pint-sized girl, with smoky grey eyes, and hair the colour of a fox's fur in the rain filled his mind; a girl, moreover, who had kicked him in the shin, and threatened to throw a glass of wine over his head! Come to think about it, his personal life had been in an uproar from the moment he'd first met her!

No doubt his secretary, Karen, in light of her view that his life lacked surprise and spontaneity, would consider Darcy's unpredictability to be good for him. She would be wrong! He wasn't at all comfortable with the twists and turns things were taking at the moment.

'You're frowning again, Logan,' his mother remarked at his side as he drove them both to the hotel where they were to meet Darcy for afternoon tea, Logan having picked her up from her apartment ten minutes earlier.

'If I am it's because I do not appreciate being dragged into the complexities of your personal life,' he clipped. After years of avoiding his mother's turbulent private life, he was not amused at being thrust into the centre of it in this way.

His mother shrugged. 'You arranged this meeting, Logan, not I.'

'Because Darcy asked me to, and for no other reason.'

'Hmm,' his mother murmured thoughtfully. 'I may have asked you this before, but—just how well do you know Daniel's daughter?'

He gave her a cold glance. 'I don't,' he snapped—at once assaulted with the memory of Darcy in his arms, of the naked softness of her body.

His mother looked puzzled. 'You told me the other day that the two of you are friends.'

'Were,' he corrected. 'And even then that was probably too strong a description of our relationship. Since you came into the equation, an armed truce is probably a better way of describing how Darcy views things between us.'

'Yet you were the one she asked to set up this meeting between the two of us,' his mother said slowly.

'Only because her father didn't stay around long enough to do it himself!' Logan pointed out.

His mother swallowed hard. 'I hurt Daniel very badly when I broke our engagement.'

'Then why did you do it?' Logan exploded.

'What choice did I have, when you refused to help me?' his mother told him bluntly.

Logan's hands tightly gripped the steering wheel. 'Don't turn this around on me—'

'I'm not, Logan.' She sighed, reaching out to lightly touch his arm. 'I'm just pointing out that I did tell you what I intended doing if Darcy couldn't be talked round. Daniel wasn't willing for me to meet her. And you refused to help me...' She paused. 'There seemed no other way.'

'You could have done what you usually do—blast away and not worry who gets mown down in the process,' he said nastily.

His mother looked at him, with a sad expression. 'One day, Logan, I hope that you and I might be able to sit down and talk over the past like the two adults we now are. I said "one day", Logan,' she inserted firmly as he would have made a deriding reply. 'So,' she asked briskly. 'Daniel tells me that Darcy is a level-headed, kind-hearted young lady; what's your opinion?'

Logan was so taken aback by the unexpectedness of the question that, for a few moments, he wasn't able to formulate an answer. Even when he did, it wasn't an answer he could give to his mother! Because he found Darcy tempestuous, not level-headed, and as for kind-hearted—! Anyway, the state of Darcy's heart, kind or otherwise, was something he didn't want to know about!

'My opinion is that you wait until you meet her and judge for yourself,' he replied noncommittally as he drove down to the basement car park of the hotel.

Maybe having his mother around for this meeting with Darcy wasn't such a bad thing after all, he decided, after taking one look at Darcy as she sat in the hotel lounge waiting for them to arrive.

Why had he never thought her beautiful? Today, in a bright red trouser suit—that should have clashed with that vivid red hair, but somehow didn't—teamed with a black blouse, both fitting the slenderness of her body perfectly, and her hair loose and gleaming down to her shoulders, her eyes huge, lashes thick and long, blusher colouring her cheeks, a bright red gloss on her lips, Darcy was absolutely gorgeous!

In comparison, his mother had played down the dark sensuality of her own beauty, wearing a demure grey skirt suit with a black blouse, even her make-up was less pronounced today; she wore only a light blusher on her cheeks, and a pale peach lip-gloss.

Logan had no doubts that both women had made these changes to their appearance in expectation of meeting the other. His mother he didn't give a care about; she played a role so often it was difficult to know with her what was real and what wasn't. But the effect on Logan of this totally different-looking Darcy was one of stunned silence.

Making him fully aware that it wasn't only her smiles that could render him speechless!

Maybe he could just introduce the two women and make

his excuses? Because he wasn't sure he could actually sit here, with his mother on one side of him, and Darcy on the other, looking the way that she did, and behave normally!

But, the introductions over, instead of making his excuses and leaving, he found himself sitting down with the two women, even agreeing to take tea with them when the waiter came over to take their order!

Will-power, Logan, he told himself disgustedly. Quite—wherever was it?

But he very quickly realised as the two women looked warily at each other that it was going to be up to him to break this initial awkward silence.

'Were you busy at lunch-time today?' he asked Darcy conversationally.

She seemed relieved to speak to him, hardly seeming to be able to even look at Margaret. 'Not too bad.'

Logan wasn't altogether sure he believed her; she still looked very tired to him. 'Have you heard from your father?' he asked.

'No,' she answered flatly, shooting his mother a brief look beneath lowered lashes.

Obviously she was wondering if Margaret had heard from Daniel Simon, Logan realised disgustedly. Well, if Darcy wasn't going to ask her, he was!

He looked at his mother with narrowed eyes. 'What about you?' he pressed.

Margaret Fraser took her time answering, crossing one slender leg over the other, before looking up at him with unemotional blue eyes. 'Logan, I— Ah, tea.' She smiled up at the waiter as he began to place tea things on the table in front of them.

The young waiter—predictably!—couldn't take his eyes off Margaret as he went about his duties, obviously wondering if this really could be the beautiful actress Margaret Fraser, but he was too polite to actually ask.

Logan viewed the young man's reaction with a totally jaundiced eye. He had been seeing this reaction to his mother's looks all his life, had found it to be the height of embarrassment when introducing her to schoolfriends, followed by university friends—the fact that she was old enough to be *their* mother making no difference! Old or young, men were always bowled over by the way his mother looked.

Darcy, he could see, looked slightly green as she also noted the young man's response to Margaret Fraser.

'Shall I pour the tea?' his mother offered lightly once they were alone again.

She could damn well answer his question, was what she could do!

'Go ahead,' he told his mother dryly. 'And while you're at it, tell us whether or not you've heard from Daniel.'

Was it his imagination, or did his mother's grasp of the teapot tremble slightly as he repeated the question...?

If it did, she quickly brought it back under control, graciously leaning forward to hand Darcy her cup of tea. But Logan wasn't fooled for a minute; his mother might be a wonderful actress, but he had known her too long to be taken in!

'Well?' he pressed again once she had given him his own cup of tea.

His mother gave Darcy a small smile. 'He was like this as a child, you know,' she remarked. 'Dogged!' She shook her head. 'He had learnt to walk by the time he was nine months old, could talk by the time—'

'Mother!' Logan interrupted her, heated colour on the hardness of his cheeks. 'I'm sure Darcy has absolutely no interest in hearing when I walked, talked, or, indeed, any of those other normal childhood achievements!'

His mother raised dark brows. 'Is it my imagination or are you a trifle tetchy today, Logan?'

A trifle—! One day he really was going to wring her neck for her! 'No, it isn't your imagination, Mother,' he bit out through gritted teeth. 'As I have already explained to you, I do not appreciate being dragged into this mess!'

'Then, my dear Logan,' his mother returned calmly, putting one slender hand on his arm, 'why don't you just leave Darcy and I to it? I'm sure we both appreciate the fact that you're a busy man. I can easily get a taxi back later. I'm sure we can manage without you—can't we, my dear?' She turned to Darcy.

Logan also turned to Darcy. He was only here because of her, and he didn't appreciate being dismissed by his mother as if he were some errand boy who had completed his job! If Darcy now did the same thing—!

Darcy pulled a face. 'I'm sorry, Logan, I really didn't think... Of course you must go. I'm sure you have other things you need to do.'

'Fine.' He slammed his teacup down on the table before standing up. 'I'll leave, then.' Without waiting for further comment from either of them he turned and strode out of the hotel.

To blazes with the pair of them! He had done as Darcy had asked him, his mother had accepted him accompanying her to the hotel, and now he had been dismissed by both of them!

He was so angry he almost forgot he had driven here, that his car was still parked in the basement of the hotel. Which only served to increase his anger; between the two of them, his mother and Darcy were making a complete mess of his ordered life—and him!

*   *   *

Darcy watched Logan leave with a certain amount of dismay, concerned that he had left in a temper, and not exactly relishing the idea of being alone with his mother, either. But, by the same token, she didn't think the two of them would talk frankly with Logan present, which was something they needed to do.

'I shouldn't worry too much about Logan,' his mother cut gently into her thoughts. 'He has a hot temper—which he hates. Logan likes to be in control, you see,' she explained affectionately. 'But a temper is often something beyond our control. However, as I said, don't worry, his temper is hot, but it quickly goes cold again.'

It seemed quite strange to be sitting here discussing Logan with someone who knew him so intimately; not only did Margaret know when he had walked and talked, she had also been the one to care for his every need as a baby. It was hard to envisage a totally helpless Logan…!

'I'm not worried,' she assured Margaret. 'I'm just a bit sad that he seems to be angry with both of us.'

His mother laughed. 'I'm used to it; Logan has been angry with me most of his life, for one reason or another. But I can see how it would be upsetting for you,' she said almost questioningly.

Because she wondered just how close Darcy and Logan were…?

Darcy wished she knew the answer to that herself. Last night— Better to forget last night, she instantly berated herself. But even today, Logan had telephoned his mother and set up this meeting, as Darcy had asked him to, had driven his mother here. That didn't seem like the actions of a man who was completely indifferent to her.

She had even dressed up today, was wearing more make-up than she usually did, in the hope of showing herself in a different light to Logan. Too often he had seen her as a weeping mess, or hot and tired from working in the kitchen; she had wanted to show him that she wasn't always like that. For all the notice he had taken of her chic appearance today she might as well not have bothered!

Darcy gave a dismissive shrug. 'He's been very kind,' she answered Margaret Fraser noncommittally.

'Hmm, most unLoganlike,' his mother offered thoughtfully. 'Oh, don't misunderstand me, Darcy,' she continued. 'I think my son is a pretty wonderful man: kind, caring, considerate, very much the gentleman. It's just that, usually, he tends to hide it very well.'

Darcy couldn't help it; she smiled. It was such an accurate description of the man she had come to know this last week that she couldn't do anything else. Logan was all of the things his mother said he was, and he really didn't like people to realise that.

'That's better.' Margaret smiled back warmly, leaning forward to pick up the plate of delicacies that had arrived with their tea. 'Have a cake, Darcy,' she invited. 'We can both think about our waistlines tomorrow!'

Margaret Fraser didn't look as if she needed to think about hers at all, slender but shapely. But then, neither did Darcy normally—so she took one of the offered cakes, a nice gooey, chocolatey one.

'We couldn't do this in front of Logan,' Margaret continued before biting into the chocolate éclair she had chosen. 'There's simply no way of eating a fresh-cream cake with any degree of ladylike delicacy!' she said, before dabbing with a napkin to remove some of the excess cream from her mouth. 'I love your father very much, you know, Darcy.'

The remark was so unexpected Darcy almost choked over her second bite of chocolate cake!

They had been talking about waistlines and cakes, for goodness' sake; where had that last remark come from:

She looked across at the older woman, finding Margaret looking straight back at her, her gaze steady and direct, all pretence totally gone as that gaze revealed the full extent of her emotions.

This woman really did love her father...

Darcy swallowed hard before moistening her lips. 'Logan asked you a question before he—left,' she began slowly. 'Do you know where my father is?'

Margaret's gaze didn't waver. 'Yes.'

Darcy's breath left her in a relieved sigh. 'Is he okay?'

Again Margaret met her gaze head on. 'Yes.'

Darcy nodded. 'That's all I need to know.'

Margaret smiled slightly. 'Can you imagine Logan accepting my answers as easily?'

'No,' Darcy answered honestly. 'But then, he doesn't have the same interest in my father's welfare that I do.'

'No.' Logan's mother sighed. 'Logan's interest, unfortunately, is much closer to home. I made a bad second marriage,' Margaret enlarged at Darcy's questioning look.

She frowned. 'I don't think—'

'It's relevant, Darcy,' the older woman told her quietly. 'Logan was eleven when his father died, twelve at the time I remarried—not a good age for any boy to be presented with a stepfather!' She looked sad. 'More to the point, he disliked Malcolm intensely. What I wasn't aware of, for some time, was that the dislike worked both ways. My husband Malcolm, without my knowledge, was an absolute brute to Logan. So much so that when he was fourteen, Logan informed me that he hated my husband, and me, and moved to Scotland to live with his grandfather. It took me several more years of being married to Malcolm before I realised exactly why Logan had gone. By which time our own relationship had been irrevocably damaged. He's never forgiven me,' she concluded sadly.

Darcy really didn't think they should be discussing Logan in this way, and yet a part of her wanted to know, wanted to try and fathom what made Logan the man that he was. The things Margaret had told her already answered some of the questions she had about him. His willingness to help her, for one thing; he obviously knew exactly what she was going through at the thought of her father's second marriage.

Except, because of the little time she had spent talking to her, Darcy didn't think she was going to hate Margaret Fraser...

'He was a child still,' Darcy excused Logan's behaviour.

Margaret shook her head in disagreement. 'Adulthood, unfortunately, hasn't changed our relationship. As far as Logan is concerned, I let him down when he needed his mother the most.' She stared Darcy right in the eye. 'Which is precisely why I won't come between you and your father.'

Darcy had already realised that. But she wasn't the child Logan had been at his mother's remarriage; she was twenty-five years old, far too old to have any say in her father's life any more. Besides, now that her initial shock at the idea had dissipated, maturity meant she simply couldn't be that selfish.

'Daniel told me that, if the two of us ever met in the right circumstances, I would like you,' Margaret said hesitantly. 'He was right.'

Darcy drew in a shaky breath. 'He told me the same thing about you,' she admitted gruffly. 'And, again, he was right. When you next speak to him, would you please tell him—?'

'Why don't you tell him yourself?' Margaret suggested

warmly. 'After he telephoned me yesterday I— It was very difficult when Logan called for me earlier. You see—your father is at my apartment, Darcy,' she admitted awkwardly. 'I couldn't bear it when I knew how deeply upset he was, and so I—'

'It's all right, Margaret,' Darcy cut in happily. And it was—she was just relieved to know where her father was. 'Does he know the two of us are meeting this afternoon?'

'I didn't tell him,' Margaret confirmed. 'He would probably have insisted on coming with me if I had, and— Can you imagine Logan's reaction to that?' she said knowingly.

After witnessing the way he behaved towards his mother, and hearing his anger directed towards her father—yes, she could imagine only too well!

'Do you think my father is likely to suffer a heart attack if I arrive back with you now?' she prompted lightly.

'Probably.' Margaret laughed softly. 'But he'll quickly get over that when—' She broke off.

'When…?' Darcy prompted.

Margaret gave a small smile. 'I was being presumptuous, jumping two steps ahead.'

'Because you believed I would give my blessing on your marriage to my father?' Darcy easily guessed. 'That isn't being presumptuous, Margaret; I should never have objected in the first place. Even if you were absolutely awful—which you aren't,' she added hastily.

'I wish you could convince Logan of that,' Margaret told her almost wistfully.

Logan!

It wasn't just a possibility now that he might be her stepbrother—it was a fact!

How on earth was he going to react to knowing that…?

CHAPTER NINE

LOGAN had no idea what he was doing standing outside the entrance of Chef Simon at eleven-thirty in the morning!

When he'd left his mother and Darcy at the hotel yesterday he had been absolutely furious at what he deemed to be their dismissal of him, had had no intention of talking to either of them again in the near future. But as the hours had passed, and he hadn't heard a word from either of them, that anger had changed to a burning curiosity.

Had the two women ended up hating each other, or had they actually come to some sort of truce? He could perfectly well understand if Darcy disliked his mother, but he would find it most unlikely that his mother could have disliked Darcy; apart from the fact she had kicked him in the shin, and threatened to throw wine over him, she was far too nice for anyone to actually dislike!

Apart from the fact—!

Logan stopped that thought. Knowing Darcy had certainly never been dull.

But if the two women hadn't ended up hating each other, they must have reached some sort of agreement over the situation. And Logan wanted to know exactly what that agreement was.

But he wasn't curious enough to put himself through another meeting with his mother. So he had come to the restaurant at a time when he knew it wasn't actually open, but Darcy would be busy in the kitchen preparing for the lunch-time trade.

He could see someone moving about inside the closed

restaurant now, although, with the room still unlit, he couldn't actually see who it was.

Oh, well, faint heart, and all that—

No, that wasn't right, he thought darkly. He wasn't here to win Darcy; he just wanted to know what was going on.

His initial knock on the door heralded no response, and so he knocked louder the second time. This time there was the sound of movement inside, the key turning in the lock seconds later, the bolt shifted back, before the door slowly opened.

'I'm sorry, but we don't open until— You!' Daniel Simon's polite smile faded rapidly as he incredulously recognised Logan.

No more incredulously than Logan recognised the other man. He had been expecting to see Darcy, or maybe one of the waitresses; he certainly hadn't expected to see the owner of the restaurant, Darcy's own father, opening the door!

Logan's mouth twisted mockingly. 'You're back, then,' he said derisively.

Daniel Simon raised blond brows. 'Obviously,' he drawled.

'And not before time,' Logan responded harshly. 'Darcy has been run off her feet in your sudden absence,' he added critically.

Daniel Simon's mouth tightened. 'I believe that is between my daughter and myself.'

'I disagree. You—'

'Logan, exactly what is it you want?' the other man interrupted curtly.

He drew in a sharp breath. The last thing he had expected had been to be confronted by Darcy's father. But, nevertheless, he wasn't about to be put off doing what he had come here to do.

'To speak to Darcy,' he told the older man abruptly.

Daniel Simon nodded, opening the door wider so that Logan could enter the strangely quiet restaurant. 'She's in the kitchen,' he supplied shortly. 'Oh, and Logan…?' he said as Logan strode past him on his way to the kitchen.

Logan stopped, turning slowly. 'Yes?' he replied arrogantly.

The chef's expression had softened. 'Don't do or say anything to upset her, hmm?' he suggested, his tone implying Logan would have him to deal with if he did so.

'*Me* upset her—!' Logan exploded. 'I like that! I don't believe I'm the one who only days ago calmly dropped the bombshell of his remarriage on her over the breakfast table. Neither am I the one—'

'Logan, again, that is between Darcy and myself,' Daniel Simon said sharply. 'But while we're on the subject of your mother—'

'We weren't,' Logan told him flatly, his hands clenched at his sides. He was beginning to wish he had never met any of the Simon family!

The other man wasn't about to be put off. 'Yes, we were,' he insisted firmly. 'And isn't it time you gave her a break? Or do you intend to hold it against her for ever that she made a mistake in her second marriage?'

Logan's mouth thinned angrily; how dared his mother discuss him—and his feelings!—with this man? 'What was it you said to me a few moments ago?' he returned icily. 'I believe that is between my mother and myself!' With one last glaring look at the older man Logan continued on his way to the kitchen.

Darcy was standing with her back towards the do when he entered the kitchen, working at one of the ta' in the centre of the room. The door closed with a swi noise behind him alerting her to the presence of another person.

'Could you bring me some eggs from the fridge?' she asked without turning.

There was a large refrigerator against the wall a short distance from the door and, after a brief look inside, Logan was able to locate a box of a dozen eggs, moving to place them down on the table beside Darcy.

'Thanks. I—' She came to an abrupt halt, having looked up and seen Logan standing beside her. 'I'm sorry, I though you were my father...' She gasped, colour instantly brightening her cheeks.

Logan's expression tightened at the mention of her father. 'Hardly,' he said sardonically. 'When did he get back?'

'Last night,' she answered awkwardly. 'I—do you mind if I carry on preparing this?' She indicated some concoction she was constructing in a saucepan. 'Only we need it for lunch, you see, and—'

'Darcy, you're waffling,' he interrupted, glad to see someone else being disconcerted for a change; he had been taken by surprise so many times the last few days, and it wasn't an emotion he was comfortable with.

'Actually...' she smiled slightly '...it's a lemon meringue pie. Not a waffle,' she explained.

'Very funny,' he returned dryly, leaning back against the table. 'You seem happy today?'

After all, the fact that Daniel Simon was back in his restaurant did not mean that everything was back to normal...

'You've seen my father?' She was busy separating eggs
v.

ery efficiently, too, Logan noted. 'He was the one who

let me in,' he explained. 'Is he back for good, or just until you can get someone else in to help you?'

Which didn't fool Darcy for a moment, he could see, as she gave him a knowing sideways glance. But *when* was someone going to tell him exactly what was going on?

Darcy picked up a saucepan and placed it on the hot-plate, deftly adding the ingredients she needed. 'Why don't you just ask what you really want to know?' she mused.

Because, after arriving here and finding Daniel Simon back at the restaurant, Logan wasn't a hundred per cent sure he knew what that was any more!

He gave Darcy a considering look. 'And just what might that be?' A wonderful tangy smell of lemons came from inside the saucepan now as the ingredients heated.

Her mouth quirked. 'Did your mother and I manage to get through tea together yesterday without scratching each other's eyes out!'

'Well—did you?' He leant back against one of the kitchen units, arms folded across his chest as he waited for her answer.

Again Darcy gave him a sideways glance. 'I'm happy to report there are no physical injuries,' she finally answered.

Except to his pride, it seemed; his feelings of being a dismissed servant yesterday, when assured by both women that they could manage without him, had not abated!

He nodded abruptly, that same pride precluding him asking for more information on how that meeting between Darcy and his mother had gone. 'And your father?' he pressed. 'Exactly where did he come from?'

'I didn't ask,' Darcy answered quietly, still busily stirring the contents of the saucepan.

'You didn't—! Whyever not?' Logan exclaimed.

Given the same circumstances, it would have been the first thing he would have wanted to know!

She shrugged. 'Because it's none of my business.' Satisfied with the consistency, she put the hot saucepan on a rack to let the contents cool.

Logan didn't agree with her. But one look at her determinedly set features told him it would be useless to pursue the point; Darcy could be as stubborn as him if the occasion merited it.

He drew in a deep breath. 'Okay,' he said tautly. 'Let's try this from another angle. What—?' He broke off as a buzzer sounded behind him.

'Excuse me for a moment, Logan.' Darcy moved deftly around him to open an oven door and take out a dozen or so individual pastry cases. 'Perfect,' she said with satisfaction after checking the pastry.

Logan frowned as he watched her. 'Are all the desserts made on the premises too?'

'Of course.' Darcy gave him a scandalised look. 'Any chef who has pride in his—or her—work wouldn't dream of serving bought desserts.'

Despite the fact that Darcy had chosen to move to a different career, it was rapidly becoming obvious to Logan that she was actually an excellent cook. Coupled with her immense loyalty and warmth of personality, that meant she was going to make some lucky man a wonderful wife one day—

Where on earth had that come from? What did it matter to him what sort of wife Darcy was or was not going to be?

'Could you just excuse me for a few minutes while I ut on the electric beater to whisk up these egg-whites?' rcy didn't even wait for his answer, pushing the switch, the noisy drone of the beater making it impossible to make further conversation.

Not that Logan particularly minded—he was still stunned by the strange direction his thoughts had just taken!

He had come here today simply to put his mind at rest concerning Darcy's meeting yesterday with his mother. Well, he could see that Darcy looked, and sounded, just fine, so he had no further reason to stay.

Except, she hadn't really told him anything...

'There.' The silence in the kitchen was gratifying as Darcy switched off the beater. 'Now, can I get you a cup of coffee?' she invited lightly. 'I can finish the lemon meringues in a few moments,' she explained easily, smiling at him brightly. 'Oops.' She grimaced as she obviously saw the way his expression tightened. 'I forgot I'm not supposed to smile at you!'

Logan could have kicked himself for so plainly reacting to that smile that Darcy couldn't help but notice it. It was time he got himself out of here. And stayed out!

'I'll pass on the coffee, if you don't mind,' he refused coldly. 'I only wanted to confirm that there were no repercussions from your meeting yesterday.' He moved away from the work unit. And Darcy. 'Everything appears to be back to normal,' he pronounced.

In fact, everything was so normal—Daniel Simon back in his restaurant, father and daughter obviously reconciled—that Logan was decidedly in the way.

How he felt it!

Darcy looked at him with dismay now. Without Logan's help in meeting his mother—albeit reluctantly!—the situation between her father and herself could still be termed as one of armed warfare. The least she owed Logan was a cup of coffee. At most, she probably owed him an explanation of exactly what had taken place yesterday after his departure from the hotel. In fact, it would probably be better—for everyone!—if she were the one to tell him that!

'Please stay for coffee, Logan,' she pressed. 'It's already made, I only have to pour it.' She indicated the perculator of coffee being kept hot on one of the worktops.

As she watched him, it was obvious Logan was having an inner battle with himself. No doubt a part of him was still angry with both Darcy and his mother. But the other part of him, the part that had compelled him to come here at all today, really wanted to know what was going on. As his mother had already stated, Logan was not a man who felt comfortable when he wasn't one hundred per cent in charge of a situation, and this one was well out of his hands. More so than he could even imagine!

'Okay. Coffee,' he finally agreed tersely. 'But I can't stay long,' he stated determinedly as she moved to pour the steaming brew into two mugs. 'I have a luncheon appointment at one o'clock.'

In other words, get on with it, Darcy, because I've already wasted enough of my precious time on this ridiculous situation!

Which was probably fair enough, she conceded ruefully. But another part of her couldn't help wondering who his luncheon appointment was with. It wasn't one of the business lunches he occasionally held at his office; she would have seen the booking for that. Which suggested it wasn't a business lunch at all...

So could his one o'clock appointment be with a woman?

After all, Logan might have kissed her—more than once—but those occasions had been spur-of-the-moment things and not the culmination of having spent an evening together. Which meant there might already be a woman in Logan's life…

Somehow Darcy found the thought of that an unpleasant one. As were her thoughts of Logan dining with another woman. Logan spending time with another woman. Logan kissing another woman. Logan in bed with another woman…!

That last vision made her feel physically sick!

Indeed, she was so shaken by it, she had to put the mugs of coffee back on the work surface, her hands shaking so much she was in danger of spilling the hot liquid all over the floor if she attempted to carry them over to the table where Logan sat waiting for her.

When had it happened?

Why had it happened?

Because she had just made the earth-shattering discovery—for her!—that she was in love with Logan McKenzie. The very last man she should ever have fallen in love with…!

What had she once so scathingly said to Logan concerning her father's feelings for Margaret Fraser? How can anyone possibly fall in love in just three weeks; she seemed to have done the same thing herself where Logan was concerned, in only a few days!

Oh, dear, he must never know of it, never even begin to guess how stupid she had be—

'I thought you said this wasn't going to take long?' Logan snarled now at her delay in producing the offered coffee.

Darcy drew in a deep controlling breath before picking up the coffee-mugs and walking over to the table. After all, she might have just made a discovery that was in danger of rocking her whole world, but Logan wasn't aware of it. And he must never be!

She simply couldn't bear it if Logan were ever to realise how she felt about him. From what she already knew of Logan, and his feelings regarding love, he was likely to run a mile if he even half guessed that she was in love with him. In the circumstances, that just wasn't possible…!

'Biscuit?' she offered, not quite able to look at him yet, suddenly shy in the realisation that if she never saw this man again she would be absolutely devastated.

Although again, in the circumstances, that wasn't very likely, either. But to watch him through the years, perhaps even witness him making one of those loveless marriages he had talked about, was surely going to be even more painful than never seeing him again?

Darcy sat down abruptly at the table opposite him. How could she have been so stupid as to fall in love with Logan, of all people?

'Apparently not,' he dryly refused her offer of a biscuit, his gaze mocking now. 'So, what did you think of my mother?'

Attack always seemed to be Logan's own form of defence; perhaps it would be as well if she were to adopt that attitude herself towards him in future.

She straightened, looking unflinchingly into the mockery of those deep blue eyes. 'I thought she was gracious, charming, obviously very beautiful—'

'Let's forget the general—totally unknowledgeable—consensus, shall we?' Logan interrupted harshly. 'What did you think of her?' His gaze was narrowed now.

Darcy hesitated. 'You aren't going to like this…'

His mouth twisted. 'She took you in!' he realised scornfully. 'She gave you the forlorn, poor misunderstood woman act, and you fell for it!' he exclaimed with a disgusted shake of his head.

Darcy bit back her own angry retort with effort. The

two of them ending up in a slanging match, over something of which they had absolutely no control, was ridiculous.

'Not completely,' she assured Logan.

The two women might have eaten cream cakes together like giggling schoolgirls, Darcy might have accepted that Margaret Fraser did genuinely love Darcy's father, but that did not mean she wasn't quite capable of knowing the other woman had her faults, that she was far from perfect. Or did he think that, as his mother, Margaret Fraser should be? It wasn't a very realistic view if he did believe that. Even Darcy, who absolutely worshipped her father, didn't expect him to be infallible.

Logan gave an impatient shake of his head. 'I can't believe you let her fool you,' he said almost angrily.

Darcy leaned forward over the table. 'Logan, what I did or didn't think of your mother is not important,' she told him softly. 'It isn't my opinion that counts,' she reasoned, having come to that conclusion all too painfully herself over the last few days.

He didn't look convinced. 'Don't tell me, your father, even though she's broken their engagement, still thinks she's wonderful!'

'My father,' she began slowly, 'is far from the stupid man you take him to be.' And far from the besotted widower she had believed him to be, too!

She and her father had talked long into the night after Darcy had accompanied Margaret Fraser back to her apartment, and Darcy was utterly sure now that he knew exactly what he was doing, that he loved the other woman in spite of her faults. As the actress obviously loved him in return.

She moistened dry lips, swallowing hard before she began speaking, aware even now that, at almost twelve o'clock, her father should really have returned to th kitchen by now, that he was deliberately allowing her this time alone with Logan. 'Logan, the engagement is very much back on,' she informed him gently. 'In fact, the two of them are going to be married—'

'You can't be serious!' he cut in incredulously.

'Perfectly,' Darcy affirmed.

He gave a disgusted snort. 'That is not a word I ever associate with my mother!'

Darcy sighed, wishing there were some way she could help alleviate the pain he had known in the past that had caused him to feel this way about his mother. But at the same time knowing, as Margaret Fraser did herself, that until Logan was receptive to what she wanted to say to him concerning the past, that she, and Darcy, would be wasting their breath.

'Nevertheless, the two of them are going to be married,' she continued determinedly.

His gaze was glacial now. 'I hope you aren't expecting me to offer them my congratulations?'

She shook her head sadly. 'I think that might be expecting a bit much,' she conceded.

'But no doubt you've given them yours',' he guessed. 'And—don't tell me—you're going to be a bridesmaid!' he scorned.

Darcy drew in a quick breath. 'Logan, has no one ever told you that bitterness is simply a form of self-destruction? That—'

'I believe I have already made my views on your amateur psychology more than plain,' he cut in coldly.

'Oh, yes, Logan, you can be assured you've made your views on several subjects more than plain!' She was becoming angry herself now. 'But it just so happens you aren't a primary player in this particular situation. As I'm not.' Something she had learnt all too painfully over the last couple of days! 'So, like mine, your opinion is not of particular importance to either your mother or my father.'

'In other words, our parents are going to marry each other, with or without our blessing,' Logan acknowledged hardly.

Darcy nodded. 'But they would obviously rather it was with.' She looked at Logan expectantly.

He remained impassive. 'You might feel prepared to play happy families, Darcy,' he told her. 'But I am not.'

She looked across at him with narrowed eyes, her frustration with this situation rapidly rising. 'Meaning?'

'Meaning they will have to get married without my blessing. In fact, as I have no intention of attending the wedding, they will have to get married without my being present at all!'

He was so obstinate, so stubborn, so uncompromising! What was it really going to cost him to be present at his own mother's wedding? Nothing as far as she could see. Unless he considered his own personal pride more important than wishing the older couple well?

Nevertheless, she tried one last time to reach him. 'Logan, you're being unreasonable—'

The loud slamming down of his empty mug interrupted her, Logan's own expression one of fury now. 'I don't see what's in the least unreasonable about it. I certainly wasn't present at my mother's first wedding—'

'You weren't even born!' At least, she presumed he wasn't...?

'Correct,' he confirmed icily. 'But I was very much alive when her second marriage took place, and, as she and Malcolm sneaked off to be married and told the family about it afterwards, I didn't attend that one either. I see absolutely no reason to break the habit of a lifetime!'

Darcy stood up, two spots of angry colour in her

erwise pale cheeks. 'You're not twelve years old now, Logan.'

He remained in his seat. 'No matter how old I was, my answer would still be the same.'

Darcy breathed hard in her frustrated anger towards this man. 'Logan, Meg and my father have asked me to be one of their witnesses at the wedding—'

'How nice for you!'

'They would like it very much if you would agree to be the other one!' she burst out.

'In their dreams!' Logan remained unmoved.

'I—you—'

Logan leant back in his chair, a half-smile curving his lips. 'So now you can report back to both of them that their little ploy in getting you to be the one to ask me didn't work,' he told her contemptuously.

Darcy saw red at that. Neither her father nor Margaret Fraser had so much as suggested she should do that—she had done it because she'd thought Logan might have been less insulting in his answer to her than he would either of them. She had been wrong!

'You are the most unforgiving, pigheaded man I have ever had the misfortune to meet!' Her voice shook with rage, her hands clenched into fists at her sides.

Again, Logan looked unmoved by her outburst. 'And you, my dear Darcy, are the most naively gullible young lady *I* have ever met,' he returned with insulting coolness.

She didn't think, didn't reason, reacted purely on instinct, which told her to pick up the bowl of recently whisked egg-whites—and put it over the top of Logan's head!

Then, as he slowly removed the bowl and placed it care-
'ly back on the table-top, the fluffy egg-whites slowly
ealing on his hair and face, Logan's expression

through the gooey mess one of stunned surprise, Darcy could only stare at him in horror for what she had just done.

She had done some terrible things to him in the short time she had known him, but Logan was never going to forgive her for this one.

Never!

CHAPTER TEN

'WILL you just get a grip, Fergus? It wasn't in the least bit funny!' Logan glared across the restaurant table—not Chef Simon!—at his cousin, as the other man seemed incapable of stopping his laughter.

· 'I'm sorry!' Fergus finally gasped. 'I can't help it! I just—my goodness, I bet you looked a sight with all that uncooked egg-white all over you!' Fergus went off into paroxisms of laughter once again.

Logan continued to scowl at the other man. Maybe one day he might be able to see the funny side of this himself—although he wouldn't count on it! But at this particular moment, only an hour or so after it had happened, he still didn't find it in the least funny.

He had stared up at Darcy in complete disbelief at the time, sure he'd been in the middle of one of those unbelievable nightmares one sometimes had. But the slow descent of the gooey white mess down his face had given instant lie to that hope; there was no way he could ever have imagined the cold stickiness of those egg-whites against his skin and hair!

Darcy had looked stunned herself at what she had done, staring down at him in horror. As well she might have done!

Logan wasn't a hundred per cent certain what his immediate intention had been—probably he had been about to wring her pretty little neck! But before he'd been able to do that, he'd heard the kitchen door swing open behind them.

'I thought I heard raised voices—good grief!' Daniel Simon gasped as he took in the scene, his gaze disbelieving in Logan's dishevelled appearance. 'What on earth happened?' He looked appalled as he moved further into the room.

Logan turned to the other man with glacial eyes, knowing how utterly ridiculous he must look. And exactly who was responsible for that? 'Your daughter has been proving to me yet again the danger of antagonising an unpredictable redhead,' he drawled hardly, his glacial gaze now taking in Darcy too.

She swallowed hard. 'I just—'

'Save it,' Logan rasped, standing up abruptly. 'It's time I was leaving, anyway—way past!' he added curtly, moving to pick up one of the towels from the rack, wiping off the excess egg-whites before looking straight at Daniel Simon. 'I would appreciate it if you could inform my mother there will be no necessity to send me an invitation to the wedding.'

The older man eyed him warily. 'You'll attend as one of our witnesses?'

Logan gave a scathing snort before throwing down the towel he had been using. 'I won't be attending at all. As I'm sure Darcy will be only too happy to explain to you once I've gone!' He strode forcefully towards the door. 'Besides, going on past—and present!—history,' he stormed, 'Darcy is likely to do something even more outrageous if we meet at the wedding—like stabbing me with a knife at the reception!'

'Logan!'

He turned slowly at the sound of Darcy's anguished cry. 'Yes?' he prompted icily.

She gave a self-conscious grimace. 'I'm sorry.'

'So am I,' Logan returned. 'So am I!' he repeated with pointed feeling.

She didn't try and stop him a second time, for which he was very grateful. Logan just wanted to get home now, before anyone else saw him, and shower off all trace of this stick messy.

Before meeting Fergus for their one o'clock luncheon appointment.

Unfortunately, he had still been so angry when he'd got to the luncheon restaurant that the events of the morning had just come tumbling out as the two men ate their meal. But far from sympathising with him, Fergus obviously found the whole thing hilarious!

'Oh, come on, Logan, lighten up,' Fergus sobered enough to advise. 'If it had happened to someone else you would be laughing about it too,' he reasoned.

'But it didn't happen to someone else,' Logan grated, still not in a mood to be reasoned with. Darcy Simon had humiliated him for the last time!

His cousin shook his head, still smiling. 'I have to say I wasn't particularly impressed when I met Darcy the other evening. She looked a plain little thing to me,' he opined as Logan looked across at him, brows raised questioningly. 'But further acquaintance might be interesting; there's obviously a lot more to Darcy than initially meets the eye!'

Logan had thought Darcy plain to look at too when he'd first met her, but somehow he did not appreciate hearing his cousin say it. Besides, he didn't see her like that any more; Darcy's inner beauty shone out of those candid grey eyes, and when she smiled—!

Logan shrugged dismissively. 'I'm sure the two of you ill have a chance to meet at my mother's wedding.' hough he couldn't say he was exactly enamoured of the of his charming, good-looking cousin becoming further acquainted with Darcy... 'I have no doubt you will receive an invitation to the wedding!' he said sarcastically.

He had no doubt that his only other male cousin, Brice, would receive an invitation too. And Brice was even more rakishly attractive than Fergus!

Damn!

Just the thought of the expletive he had first heard Darcy mutter brought the woman herself vividly to mind. As he had last seen her. A look of utter misery on her face, those deep grey eyes dark with despair at what she had just done.

Whereas, in all honesty, Logan couldn't have blamed her if she had laughed at his discomfort, as Fergus was doing now; he must have looked a sight, with that egg-white all over him. In fact, now that he could begin to think about it objectively, the whole situation had bordered on the farcical.

'That's better.' Fergus nodded his approval as Logan began to grin. 'I knew your sense of humour would kick in eventually.'

Logan's smile was rueful. 'What do you do with a woman like Darcy?' he mused.

'I have to admit I've never met one like her,' Fergus agreed. 'She sounds like a one-off to me,' he said admiringly.

Unique, Logan admitted slowly. Totally, outrageously, adorably unique.

'I think you *should* go to the wedding, Logan,' Fergus told him. 'If only to provide the other guests with a sideshow they'll never forget!' he added mischievously.

Logan was coming to the same conclusion himself concerning attending the wedding—but not for the reas Fergus stated! He simply didn't like the idea of Brice Fergus being anywhere near the emotionally vulnera' or did he mean volatile?—Darcy. The two men wer plete charmers, and, once Fergus had informed Brice of Darcy's antics where Logan was concerned, he had no doubt Brice would want to meet her too. Darcy needed protecting from herself!

At least, that was what he told himself as he drove back to his office a couple of hours later, seriously thinking of reconsidering his refusal to be a witness at the wedding. Not that his motives were exactly honourable; they had absolutely nothing to do with his mother's feelings. He simply didn't feel he could leave Darcy to the mercy of the lethal charm of his two cousins.

'Darcy Simon called three times while you were out,' Karen informed him as he entered her office that adjoined his own.

Logan came to an abrupt halt, turning slowly. 'On the telephone?' he prompted casually.

Karen gave him a quizzical look. 'Well, of course on the telephone, Logan; how else could she have called?'

After this morning, he wouldn't put anything past that particular young lady! 'You might be surprised at what Darcy can do,' he drawled. 'So Darcy telephoned?'

'Three times,' Karen confirmed.

'And?' he pressed impatiently when she didn't enlarge on the subject.

'And nothing,' Karen replied. 'The first two calls she just asked to speak to you, ringing off without leaving her name when I told her you were out to lunch. I realised it was the same caller when the third call came in only ten minutes or so ago, and this time I did get her to leave her name.'

Logan frowned. 'Does she want me to call her back?'

'She didn't say,' Karen responded. 'But she sounded a distracted, I thought,' she added helpfully.

'If she calls again, put her through, hmm?' Logan instructed before going through to his own office.

So Darcy had telephoned him three times in the last
three hours? No doubt to apologise once again. Well, she
could stew on her apology for a bit longer; he had no
intention of putting her out of her misery by returning her
calls!

Logan had told Darcy his luncheon appointment had been
for one o'clock, and at almost four o'clock, the time of
her last call, he still hadn't returned to his office. No doubt
her earlier suspicion that it wasn't a business luncheon had
been a correct one; Logan had probably been meeting the
current woman in his life.

Oh, she felt miserable, Darcy acknowledged at just after
five o'clock as she cleared away in the kitchen following
lunch. Things had been bad enough before between herself
and Logan, but she was sure he was never going to forgive
her for tipping egg-white all over him.

What on earth had possessed her to do such a thing?

She had asked herself that question a dozen or more
times since Logan had left earlier, and she still didn't have
an acceptable answer. It simply wasn't good enough that
she had been so angry with his pigheaded stubbornness
concerning attending their parents' wedding that she
hadn't been able to even think straight, had only been able
to act. She had no doubt it wasn't an excuse Logan would
accept either...!

She had no idea what she was going to say to him when
she saw him again, she only knew that she had to apologise
to him properly for what she had done to him earlie
Whether or not he would accept that apology was ano'
matter!

What a family they were going to make: mother ?

barely talking, stepson and stepfather not particularly on friendly terms either, and as for stepbrother and stepsister—! What a way for their parents to start a marriage!

'I can't ask whether or not you have a home to go to,' her father teased as he strolled back into the kitchen after checking that the dining-room was ready for this evening, 'because I know you do!'

Of course she did, she just didn't feel like going back there at the moment. Maybe Logan would return her telephone calls once he returned to his office, and if she went home she would miss him. Or maybe he would come back here himself—

And maybe pigs might fly, she told herself with a self-disgusted shake of her head.

'Just forget about it, Darcy,' her father advised after watching the different emotions flickering across the openness of her expression.

She grimaced. 'Do you think Logan has forgotten about it?' she asked miserably.

Her father smiled. 'I doubt that young man ever forgets anything,' he said with feeling. 'Look how long he's kept up his grudge against Meg.'

Logan's feelings over that situation weren't exactly a grudge, Darcy knew. He had been a young boy of twelve when his mother had remarried, an age when he'd been on the very brink of manhood, a time when he had needed his mother's love and understanding. Instead he had been given a stepfather whom he'd hated, and who had loathed him. Given his young age, the resentment Logan felt towards his mother for ever putting him in that position was erfectly understandable.

'I don't think that's quite the same thing, Daddy,' Darcy her father firmly. 'Admittedly, it was a long time ago, no less painful to Logan for all that.'

Her father raised his hands in a conciliatory gesture. 'Margaret is going to be very upset once she knows he isn't going to attend the wedding. In fact,' he said worriedly, 'she may even decide to call the whole thing off until he will agree to attend.'

Margaret Fraser was perfectly capable of doing that, Darcy knew; the other woman's own love for her son had never changed, no matter how cutting Logan might have been to her over the years. But Darcy also knew that her father couldn't bear that uncertainty a second time where the woman he loved was concerned.

It had been a painful thing for Darcy to realise that her father had fallen in love with another woman only a year after her mother had died, but she had accepted it now, and she was well aware of how much her father loved Meg and needed her as his wife.

Her father was looking thoughtful. 'Maybe Margaret doesn't have to know,' he muttered. 'You and Logan appear to have become friends, so perhaps you could try talking to him again once—'

'Oh, please, Daddy,' Darcy protested. 'Would you still have friendly feelings towards someone who had tipped egg-white all over your head?'

And cried all over him. Three times. Kicked him in the shin. Once. And threatened to throw wine all over him! Again, once...

Her father shrugged. 'That depends on what the provocation had been. In your case, I believe it was quite severe. It would also depend on whether or not I had a sense of humour,' he added critically. 'You're probably right,' he instantly conceded heavily. 'I haven't seen any evidence of a sense of humour in that particular young m let alone the ability to laugh at himself!'

'The restaurant door was unlocked, so I let myse

the young man in question drawled as he strolled arrogantly into the kitchen. 'I believe you were discussing the merits—or otherwise—of my sense of humour...?' Logan said in a dangerously soft voice, looking from one to the other of them, dark brows raised challengingly.

Was that a pig she had just seen fly past the window?

She might just as well have; the thing she had thought would never happen, Logan once again seeking her out, had actually happened—but it couldn't have been at a more inopportune moment. It took only one glance at Logan's coldly set features to know that he did not appreciate walking in here to hear himself being discussed between Darcy and her father in this way. In fact, it felt as if he were emitting shards of ice from the coldness of those deep blue eyes!

'Lack of it is a better description,' Darcy's father was the one to scathingly answer the young man. 'It's going to break your mother's heart when she knows you won't attend the wedding.'

Logan's mouth twisted. 'You have to be in possession of a heart in the first place for it to be able to break!'

'No, Daddy!' Darcy just had time to shout before her father made a lunge at the younger man, moving quickly to put a restraining hand on his arm before he could actually reach Logan.

Logan, who had remained completely unmoving as the older man had lunged at him!

Maybe he just didn't believe her father would really have hit him? Although, after her own behaviour, he should have known better! Darcy had certainly believed her father was going to strike the younger man.

Logan eyed Daniel Simon coldly now. 'It's easy to see where Darcy gets her hot temper,' he said.

'Verbally reasoning with you doesn't seem to make any impression,' her father retorted angrily.

Logan shook his head. 'At least Darcy doesn't leave her marks on me where they can be seen,' he murmured dryly. 'And I very much doubt my mother would appreciate it if one, or both, of us were to arrive at the wedding with a black eye!' he taunted the older man.

Darcy was too busy still reeling at Logan's remark about leaving her marks on him where they couldn't be seen to be able to take in the rest of what he had just said, deliberately not looking at her father as she sensed his sharp interest at the other man's remark. Damn Logan, he made it sound as if she—as if the two of them—

'Do I take it from that remark,' her father began slowly—disbelievingly, 'that you have reconsidered your previous decision not to be present at the wedding...?'

It did sound as if Logan might have done exactly that, Darcy also realised dazedly. Unbelievable as that might seem!

Logan gave an abrupt inclination of his head. 'After further thought, I have decided it would be churlish not to be your second witness,' he bit out with economic harshness.

Darcy's hand slowly dropped from her father's arm as she turned fully to look at Logan. Had he had further thought, or had the woman he'd had his over-three-hour lunch with pointed out—in a less dramatic way than Darcy had earlier—that she thought he ought to reconsider his decision, and attend his own mother's wedding? Somehow Darcy thought the latter was probably nearer the truth. And the realisation, in view of her own recently realised feelings towards Logan, that some other woman had this much influence on him made her feel thoroughly depressed.

'Well?' He was eyeing her closely now.

Darcy stiffened defensively, her own emotions making her far too vulnerable where this man was concerned. 'Well, what?' she challenged. 'Are you expecting congratulations for doing what you should have done in the first place? Because if you are—'

'Darcy!' her father cut in sharply, warningly. 'I think this is very decent of you, Logan.' He held his hand out to the younger man.

Logan shook that hand briefly. 'Just be happy, hmm,' he said gruffly.

'Oh, we will,' Daniel assured him with certainty. 'If the two of you will excuse me, I think I'll just go and tell Meg the good news.'

Neither Darcy nor Logan attempted to stop him. Logan, no doubt because, having made his decision, it was no longer of interest to him what Daniel did about it. And Darcy because—because she was still smarting from the knowledge that there was a woman in Logan's life somewhere who had this much influence over him!

'Well?' he prompted again once they were alone together in the kitchen.

What did he want—a medal? Just for agreeing to do what he shouldn't have refused in the first place? If he did, he was going to be out of luck! She—

'You telephoned my office earlier, Darcy,' he continued softly, his gaze searching on the paleness of her face. 'Three times, I believe,' he added as she made no response.

She had totally forgotten those three telephone calls during the last few amazing minutes! And in light of the fact that there was obviously a woman of importance already his life, she now felt rather foolish for having made calls at all. It looked as if she were chasing after

hrugged. 'I just wanted to apologise.'

'Again?'

Darcy looked sheepish. 'You didn't seem very receptive to the one I made earlier.'

He gave a smile. 'My ears were still full of egg-white!'

She winced at this reminder of her earlier behaviour. She just didn't know what came over her whenever Logan was around; she had certainly never behaved in this outrageous way with anyone else!

Had he told his lady-friend about her? About the awful things she had done to him since they'd first met? Oh, goodness, she hoped not! She was miserable enough already at the discovery that Logan obviously already had a romance in his life, without imagining him laughing at her antics as he related her outrageous behaviour to his girlfriend.

'How did lunch go?' Logan enquired. 'I trust the lemon meringues were a popular dessert?'

She nodded awkwardly. 'Once I had whisked up some more egg-whites to make the meringue.'

Logan laughed. 'Well, I hardly thought you were going to scrape up the remains of the first lot and use that!'

She managed a faint smile. 'There wasn't enough of it left to do that!'

He looked about them pointedly at the otherwise deserted restaurant. 'Have you finished here for now? Can I offer you a lift home?'

A lift home didn't in any way cover what she wanted from Logan!

But those wants, she knew, were going to remain unfulfilled. She hadn't stood much of a chance with Logan before, but now that she knew there was someone else i his life—someone he obviously cared about enough to tually listen to!—she knew she was completely wa her time loving Logan.

She just wished she could convince her aching heart of that!

She sighed. 'No, I don't think so, thank you, Logan,' she refused. 'It's been a long day already, I think I could do with a walk in the fresh air.'

He gave her a searching look, his own expression unreadable. 'Sure?'

She wasn't sure about anything any more—except that she loved this man!

'Sure,' she confirmed huskily, unable to meet that searching gaze. 'I—thank you for changing your mind about the wedding. As you saw, it's made my father very happy.'

Logan grimaced. 'Let's hope it has the same effect on my mother.'

'Oh, it will,' Darcy said with certainty.

Neither of them seemed to know what to say after that, the silence in the kitchen becoming unbearable to Darcy as the seconds slowly ticked by.

'I really am sorry about my behaviour earlier,' she finally burst out. 'I promise that in future—for your own safety!—I'll try to stay well out of your way,' she said miserably, knowing that she probably wouldn't see Logan again now until the wedding next month. Even then, he was likely to bring the woman he had lunched with today as his partner...!

'I don't believe you have to go that far,' Logan replied, smiling ruefully.

Darcy's own smile was bleak. 'I think it might be better.'

'For whom?' he probed sharply.

She turned away, swallowing hard. 'For both of us,' she ...vered. 'After a bit of a shaky start—all my own fault, ...it—I'm very pleased that my father and Meg are to

be married. But that—that doesn't mean we have to be—
that the two of us—'

'I see,' Logan said flatly.

Darcy looked at him sharply. Did he see? She sincerely
hoped not. It was bad enough that she knew she was in
love with him, without Logan realising it too!

But, no, there was no amusement or pity in the harsh
scrutiny of his gaze, only cold arrogance.

'I'll see you at the wedding, then,' she told him with
forced brightness.

He nodded abruptly. 'It would seem so,' he responded
tautly. 'I— Goodbye, Darcy.'

She had barely mumbled a reply to his cold dismissal
when she heard the kitchen door swing shut behind him,
quickly followed by the slamming of the restaurant door.

Darcy sat down shakily on one of the kitchen stools, her
face buried in her hands as the tears began to fall.

Logan must never know—never guess!—that she had
made her biggest blunder of their acquaintance, and fallen
in love with him!

CHAPTER ELEVEN

LOGAN sipped the champagne from his glass, eyeing the noisy family gathering belligerently. *What* was he doing here?

Stupid question; he knew exactly what he was doing here. His grandfather had been persuaded into holding an engagement party for Meg and Daniel two weeks prior to their wedding. Usually this was the type of family gathering Logan most wanted to avoid, and he would have done so, but for one thing...

But so far that one thing didn't appear to be here!

After ten days of not seeing her, Logan had mistakenly thought Darcy would be one of the guests at his grandfather's castle this weekend, that Daniel's daughter was sure to be invited. Admittedly he had only arrived himself a short time ago, his flight to Aberdeen having been delayed, meaning he had only had time to quickly shower and change before coming downstairs to join the thirty or so guests in the main salon. But they would soon be called in to dinner, and there was definitely no sign of Darcy.

It simply hadn't occurred to him that she wouldn't be at her own father's engagement party. If it had, he wouldn't have bothered to make the journey himself!

'Cheer up, Logan,' his cousin Brice advised dryly as he stood at his side, the two of them making a formidable pair, both darkly handsome, but Brice's eyes green where Logan's were blue. 'It might never happen!'

He wasn't sure what had happened—he only knew that he'd missed Darcy the last ten days, had been sure that

146

he would at least see her at his grandfather's this weekend. He wished now he had asked his mother if Darcy were going to be here, and not just trusted that she would be!

He scowled. 'How soon after dinner do you think I'll be able to make my excuses and go to bed?'

Brice grinned at his obvious discomfort. 'I thought you and Aunt Meg had reached some sort of truce the last few weeks?' He raised mocking dark brows.

That might be exaggerating things slightly, although Logan accepted that he and his mother were at least giving the impression that hostilities had been suspended!

Logan put down his empty champagne glass. 'We have,' he confirmed tersely. 'But, as you very well know, I hate these sort of parties, with all the family trying to get on. And usually failing miserably!' He watched his grandfather playing the grand host to family and friends alike. It was all a sham for the latter, of course; the McDonald clan were not known for their family togetherness! 'In fact, I'm surprised to see you here this weekend, too,' he added questioningly.

Brice led a solitary existence, often disappearing off the social scene for months at a time. The fact that he was here this weekend must mean he was either between commissions or looking for inspiration.

Brice eyed him teasingly. 'I'm wondering which one of the single beauties is Darcy,' he prompted interestedly.

Logan stiffened, turning to him swiftly. 'You've been talking to Fergus!'

His cousin gave a gleeful grin. 'Bet your life I have— nothing else but the chance to meet this fiery virago would have induced *me* to come here this weekend!' He look at the glittering, chattering guests with the same dist Logan had minutes ago.

Logan retorted resentfully, 'She is not a candidate for one of your brief flings, Brice.'

His cousin raised an innocent expression. 'I didn't for a moment think she was,' he replied. 'I just wanted to meet the young lady who had got the better of my arrogantly self-assured cousin!'

'That arrogance is obviously a family trait,' Logan returned pointedly. 'And I'm afraid you're out of luck—because Darcy isn't here!' He announced this with satisfaction.

'Ah,' Brice said with feeling.

'What do you mean, "ah"?' Logan demanded suspiciously.

'Just, ah,' his cousin responded with feigned innocence.

Logan scowled once more—an expression that was becoming all too familiar with him just recently. But there didn't seem to be much to smile about any more! Oh, his business interests were still successful; they just seemed to have lost their challenge the last couple of weeks. If he was completely honest, he missed having Darcy around to threaten him, kick him, and throw things over him...

He should be pleased his life had returned to its calm predictability!

But he wasn't.

And he knew he wasn't...

His mouth set grimly. 'I—'

'If you'll excuse me, Logan,' Brice said slowly, distractedly, his gaze fixed somewhere across the crowded room. 'I've just seen someone over there who merits a second look...'

Most of the women here this evening, single or otherse, were so beautiful they merited a second look in fact, d ones too, most theatrical acquaintances of his mother. s just that none of them held any interest for Logan.

Although he thanked this particular woman, whoever she was, for distracting his cousin from a subject that was far too personal as far as Logan was concerned!

'Go ahead,' he invited affectionately. 'Which one is she?' he asked interestedly.

'She's disappeared for the moment, but—ah, a Mona Lisa with red hair...' Brice murmured before setting off determinedly across the crowded room.

Logan shook his head as he gazed indulgently after his cousin. If he was the practical, predictable one of the family, then Brice was the artistic, unpredictable one. Fergus came somewhere in between. Which was probably why the three of them always got along so well together—

A Mona Lisa with red hair...?

There was only one woman Logan could think of who could possibly fit that description. Darcy...!

Wasn't he bowled over himself every time she gave that enigmatic smile? Wasn't it a smile he had hungered for the last ten days...?

There were too many people in this room, he decided impatiently as he easily located Brice standing on the far side of the room, but couldn't see the woman his cousin was now in conversation with, Brice's dark head bent solicitously towards her much shorter height.

It had to be Darcy!

She was here, after all. He could hardly wait to—

'Logan, isn't it?' enquired a breathlessly female voice.

He turned sharply, scowling his irritation at being stopped from joining Brice and the woman he was sure now had to be Darcy. A tall blonde his mother had introduced him to earlier now stood at his side, smiling at h' engagingly.

At any other time, under any other circumstances, L knew he would have responded to the invitation

actress's smile. But not now. Now when he was sure Darcy
was even at this moment being charmed by his oh-so-
lethally fascinating cousin.

'Fiona, isn't it?' he acknowledged tersely, his attention
still across the room as he tried to catch a glimpse of the
woman Brice was talking to.

'Francesca Darwin,' the actress corrected, obviously not
too put out that he hadn't remembered her name correctly.
'I play the part of Meg's sister in the television series
we're filming at the moment,' she supplied helpfully.

Logan's brows rose. Considering this woman was only
aged in her mid-to late-twenties, Make-up must be doing
a wonderful job on his mother to make the two women
look like sisters!

'Of course,' he replied politely—having had no idea until this moment that his mother's role even involved a sister!

'She's wonderful, isn't she?' Francesca looked admiringly across the room to where Meg was smiling lovingly
at her new fiancé as the two of them talked softly together.

The statement didn't actually require an answer—and,
in all honesty, Logan didn't have one! He didn't particularly want to be having this conversation at all—would
much rather join Brice and Darcy!—let alone hear that this
beautiful young woman seemed to have nothing but ad-
miration for his mother.

Daniel Simon, a decent and honourable man, plainly
loved Meg. Darcy, straightforward and honest, had come
to like her, too. And Francesca, this young woman, who
worked with her on a daily basis, had nothing but admi-
tion for her. Could they all be wrong about Meg, and he
right? Or was he the one who was wrong…?

wever, it wasn't something he had the time to deal
st now. 'I'm sorry, Miss Darwin—'

'Francesca,' she prompted warmly. 'This castle is something else, isn't it?' she added with an admiring look round, seeming unaware that Logan was trying to make his excuses.

Something else just about described it. Logan had spent his teenage years growing up here, still considered it home, but he easily acknowledged that its splendour was magnificent.

His grandfather, as much as he was able—and with the modern central heating cunningly disguised behind other fixtures!—had filled the thirty or so rooms that comprised this sixteenth century castle with genuine antiques, armour and swords from the Scottish-English wars, huge tapestries adorning the mellow stone walls. The grounds were no less impressive, the deer his grandfather farmed taking up acres of the land, the rest given over to dense forests and streams. There was even a trout lake half a mile or so away.

'It is,' Logan agreed. 'But I really do have to—'

'Logan, I've brought someone over to say hello,' Brice cut in lightly.

Logan didn't even need to turn to know that it was Darcy; even if his senses hadn't already alerted him to the fact, he could smell the perfume he always associated with her.

She looked wonderful! A knee-length shimmering grey dress, the exact colour of her enigmatic eyes, clung lovingly to the perfection of her body, her hair a soft red curtain down to her shoulders, her eyes huge and luminous, soft colour in her cheeks, a scarlet gloss on her lips. She looked good enough to eat, and Logan suddenly found he felt surprisingly hungry!

'Logan,' she greeted huskily.

'Darcy,' he returned gruffly, his dark gaze eating her up—if nothing else could.

She looked slightly slimmer than he remembered, dark smudges beneath her eyes, eyes that appeared deeply shadowed. Despite her well-wishes to her father and his mother, wishes Logan was sure were completely genuine, he could see that Darcy was far from happy.

She was looking enquiringly at Francesca Darwin now, obviously waiting for an introduction. When all Logan wanted to do was carry her upstairs, to the privacy of one of the fifteen bedrooms, and make love to her until he had completely dispelled those shadows from her eyes!

'Francesca,' the actress introduced herself, briefly shaking Darcy's hand. 'And I believe you're—Daniel's daughter?' she asked with friendly interest.

'Yes,' Darcy confirmed stiltedly.

'Poor Darcy has been wandering around lost amongst the turrets and cellars for the last fifteen minutes or so, trying to find her way here from the North Tower.' Brice was the one to explain her late arrival indulgently, a consoling hand at one of her elbows.

Which easily explained why Darcy hadn't been down here when Logan had first arrived. But now that she had arrived, Logan found he wanted to remove Brice's hand from her arm and—

'Why didn't you tell me that your cousin was Brice McAllister?' Darcy said with soft reproval, obviously remembering that painting of Brice's hanging on the wall in Logan's apartment.

He hadn't told her his cousin was the world-renowned painter—because it hadn't occurred to him to do so. The two men had grown up together; he simply never gave it ought that Brice was McAllister. Just as he never gave 's's success as a writer any thought, either. All three men were successful in their chosen field, but to each other they were just cousins and lifelong companions.

But he could see by the reproval in the darkness of Darcy's eyes that explanation would do very little to alleviate the embarrassment she had obviously felt, at their introduction, that Brice was actually the painter of the picture of his grandfather's castle she had so admired at Logan's apartment a couple of weeks ago!

Could he never do anything right where this woman was concerned?

Logan looked wonderful!

Darcy had both dreaded and anticipated seeing him again this weekend. Anticipated, because the last ten days without so much as a sight of him had dragged interminably. Dreaded, because she had been sure the next time she saw him that it would be in the company of the woman who obviously meant so much in his life she was able to influence his decision concerning attending his mother's wedding.

Francesca...

Tall. Blonde. Sexily alluring in a fitted black dress. The other woman was everything that Darcy wasn't. Even the other woman's name was beautiful.

'Is it important?' Logan rasped harshly now.

Was what importa—? 'Well, I did feel rather silly not knowing,' she answered abruptly, realising he was referring to her earlier remark concerning his cousin.

This family were all so talented, so much larger than life. A famous actress. A multimillionaire businessman. A world-renowned painter. Even the grandfather, Hugh McDonald, with his castle, his distinguished good looks so like Logan's own, was intimidating. Darcy felt totall out of her depth in such company.

She had known this weekend in Scotland was going to be difficult, but, for her father and Meg's sake she had known she had to come here. But seeing Logan, his dark good looks a perfect foil for the blonde beauty of the lovely Francesca, she knew it was going to be even harder to get through than she had imagined. Thank goodness Brice McAllister was here on his own too, and inclined to be friendly!

'Don't give it another thought, Darcy,' Brice assured her easily now. 'Just concentrate on thinking over my earlier suggestion, hmm?' he added eagerly.

'You haven't propositioned her already, have you, Brice?' Logan put in hardly.

Darcy gave him a frowning look, heated colour in her cheeks. 'Your cousin has very kindly suggested that he would like to paint me,' she explained carefully, not liking Logan's implication at all. Although she hadn't particularly taken Brice McAllister's suggestion seriously, either, sure he was just being friendly. After all, the man was world-famous. Besides, who would ever want to buy a painting of her, even a McAllister...?

'How wonderful!' the woman Francesca gushed excitedly.

'Really?' Logan raised scornful brows. 'Is that another way of inviting her to your studio to see your etchings?' he taunted his cousin.

Darcy could feel her temper beginning to rise. Something that hadn't happened once in the ten days since she had last seen Logan. What was it about him that made her so angry all the time?

'Hardly,' Brice was the one to answer dryly, smiling down at her reassuringly. 'But if it bothers you that much, Logan, you can always come along to Darcy's sittings...?' added challengingly.

Darcy looked frowningly up at Brice. Why on earth should it bother Logan what she did? Unless Brice was simply mocking Logan's future role as her stepbrother? Well, he could forget that; she was far too old to welcome the protection of a reluctant stepbrother. Especially when that stepbrother was Logan!

It was obvious from Logan's darkly scowling expression that he did not appreciate his cousin's mockery.

They really were an extraordinarily handsome family, Logan, Fergus, and Brice, although Fergus didn't appear to be present this weekend. But Logan and Brice were enough to cope with at one time!

'I doubt that will be necessary,' Logan rasped. 'You—' He broke off as the dinner gong sounded.

Darcy breathed a sigh of relief. This meeting with Logan was turning out as difficult as she had imagined it might; they obviously had nothing to say to each other. But one look at him had told her that her feelings for him hadn't changed; she was in love with him!

But her relief was shortlived once they reached the dining-room. The volume of guests meant that there was no set seating arrangement at the long dining-table, and once Hugh McDonald and the guests of honour, Meg and Daniel, had been seated, everyone else just found a place for themselves. Darcy found herself seated with Brice McAllister on one side, and Logan on the other, Francesca on Logan's other side. Wonderful!

'How are you?' Logan said softly as the butler moved discreetly about the table filling wine-glasses.

'Very well, thank you,' she answered awkwardly, not quite able to meet his gaze, suddenly shy in the renewe realisation that she still loved him.

It hadn't been easy this last ten days, but at least had been spared seeing him and knowing she could have him. Being near him like this, Francesca at his side, was torture for her.

'You?' she asked politely.

'The same,' he replied tersely. 'Are you going to accept Brice's suggestion?'

She shook her head, smiling ruefully. 'He was only being nice.'

Logan's mouth thinned. 'Brice is never nice where his work is concerned.'

She swallowed hard, still slightly overwhelmed by the talented company she found herself in. 'I think in this case he was,' she persisted.

'Do I hear my name being taken in vain?' Brice interrupted interestedly.

Logan glanced across at his cousin, eyes a glacial blue. 'Darcy seems to think you aren't serious about your suggestion of painting her.'

'Oh, but I am,' Brice McAllister instantly assured her. 'Very serious,' he added determinedly. 'In fact, I have a feeling that Darcy's portrait will be the central focus of my next exhibition.'

'But maybe Darcy doesn't want to be painted,' Logan told him. 'Do you?' he said flatly as he turned to her.

It seemed incredible to her that an artist of Brice McAllister's calibre should even consider her a suitable subject for one of his paintings. Flattering too. But as Logan had so rightly pointed out, she wasn't sure she wanted to be on show for thousands of people to sit and look at.

Just as she didn't particularly want to be a subject of contention between the two cousins. She had hoped to remain very low-key this weekend, do her bit for her father, visually supportive of his future marriage into this family before fading back into her own world of obscurity.

Brice McAllister's interest in painting her was making that very difficult to do.

'I'm sure it's something that can be discussed another time,' she dismissed lightly. 'I believe your grandfather is about to propose a toast to the engaged couple.' She had realised this with some relief as Hugh McDonald had got to his feet at the head of the table.

As far as Darcy was concerned, the lengthy dinner that followed was not enjoyable. Oh, the food was wonderful, definitely worthy of Chef Simon's standards. It was just the company that made it unbearable for her. Despite what Logan had said about his cousin, Brice was very kind, the two of them had talked amiably together on numerous subjects. It was just Darcy's awareness of Logan talking with Francesca that made it a nightmare for her.

Would the other couple be sharing a bedroom in this vast castle later on this evening? Just the thought of it made Darcy feel physically ill. In fact, it meant she could barely eat any of the delicious food that was put before her.

'Are you on a diet?'

She turned sharply to look at Logan, realising as she did so that he had been watching her as she pushed the strawberries and cream around in her bowl, rather than eating them.

'No.' she grimaced. 'I'm just not hungry.'

He frowned. 'You didn't eat the smoked salmon or the venison, either.'

Her cheeks felt suddenly warm at the realisation that, for all she had thought him totally engrossed in the beautiful Francesca, Logan must have been watching her for some time to be aware of the fact that she hadn't actually eaten much of the food they had been served.

She shrugged. 'I'm just not very hungry.'

'You start your new job soon, don't you?' he enquired.

She was surprised he had remembered that. And, yes, she began work at the kindergarten next week.

'Nervous?' One of his hands moved to cover hers.

She hadn't been—but she was now. What was Logan doing? More to the point, what was Francesca going to think of him touching her in this way?

'You shouldn't be, you know,' Logan continued gently. 'I'm sure the children are going to love you.'

She wished that he did!

She might as well wish for the moon, and Darcy knew that even more than before after today.

She had been overwhelmed earlier this afternoon when she had arrived at the castle with her father and Meg, not even the rugged beauty of the countryside on the drive up from the airport in the hire car having prepared her for the sheer enormity of Meg's family home. The drive up from the road had seemed to take for ever, thousands of deer grazing in the fields, and as for the castle itself...!

Built of a mellow stone that seemed to have a soft orange hue to it, the main building itself was flanked by four huge turrets, genuine cannons from a sixteenth-century ship flanking each side of the main entrance. It was like something out of a fairy tale!

The inside was even more impressive, furnished with genuine antiques, most of them of a warlike nature, admittedly, but then, in earlier centuries Scotland had seen many wars. Mainly with the English!

Hugh McDonald had turned out to look like an older version of Logan, giving Darcy an idea of what Logan would look like in forty years' time—absolutely formidable!

Darcy had been allocated one of the bedrooms in the th Tower, choosing to take Hugh McDonald's suggestion that she rest until dinner-time. Not because she really needed to rest, but to give herself a chance to gather her scattered defences in anticipation of seeing Logan that evening. The story she had given Brice, of getting lost in the vastness of the castle, was a slight exaggeration; she had simply delayed coming downstairs for as long as she possibly could without missing dinner altogether. Delayed seeing Logan with the beautiful Francesca for as long as possible!

But, in truth, it had made no difference to the pain she felt at seeing him with the other woman, of having to accept Francesca's importance in his life.

Darcy gently removed her hand from Logan's grasp. 'I'm looking forward to starting work,' she assured him. For one thing, it would give her something else to think about besides him!

Logan's mouth had tightened at the removal of her hand, his gaze narrowed now. 'Then why aren't you eating?' He frowned. 'Could it be that you're still upset about Daniel and my mother?' he probed.

'No, it couldn't,' she denied instantly, her smile affectionate as she glanced down the table at the engaged couple; there was no doubting her father and Meg's genuine feelings of love for each other. 'They make a wonderful couple, don't they?' she murmured wistfully.

'Wonderful,' Logan confirmed dryly.

She glanced back at him, frowning slightly. 'But you still have your doubts…?'

'It's not really any of my business, is it?'

No, it wasn't. But his feelings towards marriage, any marriage, still dismayed her.

She glanced over to where the beautiful Francesca in conversation with the man seated to her right. Wa aware of Logan's feelings towards marriage? Dar cerely hoped so, otherwise the other woman had a terrible shock coming to her.

Although the thought of Logan married to another woman made Darcy feel faint!

She swallowed hard. 'I—'

'There's dancing in the main salon after dinner,' Logan told her abruptly.

Almost as if he had known she had been about to make her excuses and escape to her bedroom…?

'Darcy has already promised the first dance to me, old chap,' Brice interrupted brightly, taking a firm hold of Darcy's hand. 'But I'm sure she'll save one for you later on in the evening!' he added tauntingly.

Darcy turned to give Brice a quizzical glance—only to have him give her a conspiratorial wink!

Brice McAllister knew, had somehow guessed, that she was in love with Logan!

The question now was—would he tell his cousin?

All thoughts of making a hasty escape to her bedroom fled as she knew she couldn't allow Brice McAllister to do that. She would have to talk to Brice first, beg him if necessary not to tell Logan of her feelings for him. Because Logan's embarrassed pity was something she couldn't bear!

'It all sounds wonderful!' She gave Brice a big, meaningless smile, and saw a mischievous glint in his deep green eyes as he easily received and acknowledged, her message.

'Wonderful,' Logan echoed hardly. 'But I should warn you to watch out for Darcy's feet, Brice,' he mentioned with a glance in Darcy's direction.

'I'm sure she dances divinely,' his cousin complimented drily.

'It's the kicks you have to watch out for,' Logan went on.

Darcy knew exactly what he was referring to, angry colour in her cheeks. 'I'm sure Brice would never be ungentlemanly enough to insult me so that I would need to kick him!' she returned swiftly.

'I must say, Logan, I find it hard to believe you could ever be justified in being ungentlemanly to a lovely young lady like Darcy,' Brice McAllister reproved jokingly.

'All too easily, believe me,' Logan returned, his mouth a thin, angry line.

Darcy turned away so that he shouldn't see the sudden tears in her eyes. Anger was the last emotion she wanted to arouse in Logan. But anger towards each other seemed to be all that they had...

CHAPTER TWELVE

'SHE's absolutely enchanting, Logan,' Brice whispered at his side.

The two men stood in the main salon, several couples dancing in the centre of the room, Darcy and her father one of them. They made a striking couple, Daniel Simon tall and boyishly good-looking, Darcy so tiny, looking beautiful as she laughed at something her father had just said.

'She is.' Logan didn't even bother to pretend not to know who his cousin was referring to. Considering Brice had only recently finished dancing with Darcy himself, it would be slightly ridiculous to even attempt to do so!

Brice glanced at him. 'Then why don't you tell her so?'

'Now why on earth would I want to do that?'

'Because you're in love with her,' Brice stated evenly.

Logan almost choked over the champagne he had just sipped. 'I'm—I'm what?' he finally managed to burst out.

'In love with Darcy,' Brice repeated, his calmness in direct contrast to Logan's choked disbelief. 'I must say, I admire your taste. I always thought, if you ever did fall in love—and for years I've doubted it would ever happen—that it would be with someone completely unsuitable. But Darcy is unpretentious, charming, beautiful, has a great sense of humour—'

'I am not in love with Darcy!' Logan finally recovered ~ough to protest. 'I always knew that artistic side of you ⸱de you something of a romantic, Brice,' he derided. ⸱ I didn't realise it made you delusional, too!'

His cousin raised reproving brows. 'It doesn't,' he said flatly.

'Then it must be the champagne,' Logan rejoined.

'It isn't the champagne, either,' Brice replied. 'Logan, do you intend being an idiot all your life?'

'I wasn't aware that I had been,' he returned stiffly.

'You will be if you let Darcy go out of your life,' Brice warned him.

'That's hardly likely to happen,' Logan said wryly. 'In two weeks' time her father and my mother will be married. Which will effectively make us stepbrother and stepsister,' he explained at Brice's enquiring look.

Brice looked quizzical. 'And you're happy to settle for that, are you?'

Logan gave a dismissive laugh, shaking his head. 'I have no idea what you're talking about, Brice.'

'No?' Brice gave him a sceptical glance. 'You didn't like it earlier when I was holding Darcy's arm, and you looked ready to strangle me a few minutes ago when I was dancing with her.'

Damn Brice; he was too observant by half. And, no, he hadn't liked Brice being close to Darcy. But to say that he, Logan, was in love with her, was ridiculous. They had known each other only a couple of weeks, and a tempestuous couple of weeks at that. It was simply that he felt protective towards her, nothing else.

'I was merely wondering at what stage of the evening she would kick you,' Logan quipped.

Brice smiled. 'She won't.'

'Oh?' Logan was surprised. 'And what makes you exempt?'

'I only hope it isn't too late when you decide to w up, Logan,' Brice warned softly.

Logan's eyes narrowed. 'Too late for what, Bric

'She's everything I've said, and more, Logan,' Brice said. 'I can assure you, we won't be the only men to see that.'

Logan didn't like discussing Darcy in this way. And he didn't like Brice talking about her at all.

But that didn't mean he was in love with her. She had been totally vulnerable when he'd met her, still was in many ways; he just didn't like to see her hurt.

'Why don't you ask her to dance?' Brice suggested as the music came to an end and Darcy and her father returned to Meg.

Why didn't he?

'Scared, cuz?' Brice asked.

'Reverse psychology—cuz?' Logan returned bitingly. 'I'm now supposed to rush over and ask Darcy to dance just to prove you wrong—right?'

Brice was unconcerned. 'I was merely wondering why you haven't danced with your future stepsister.'

'Probably because my cousin is being such a pain in the neck about it!' Logan rasped.

'And will continue to be so until you ask Darcy to dance,' Brice assured him unrepentantly.

Logan stared at his cousin. 'Why is it so important to you?'

Brice laughed. 'It isn't important to me.'

'You could have fooled me!' Logan exclaimed.

'She dances like a dream, Logan,' Brice encouraged. 'So light in your arms, and yet so sexy at the same time. I— something wrong, Logan?' Brice said innocently as he ʒeard the slight choking noise in Logan's throat. 'Oops, late, Logan,' Brice informed him as he looked across ʒalon. 'Grandfather got to her first!'

ʒan turned in time to see his grandfather leading a

rather self-conscious Darcy onto the large area that had been cleared in the centre of the room for dancing.

At almost eighty, his hair showing only a slight salting of grey, his grandfather looked extremely handsome in his black evening suit and snowy white shirt, the slimness of his body showing no signs of age as he led Darcy nimbly around the floor in a waltz.

The two of them talked softly as they danced, Logan able to see that Darcy was slowly relaxing, moving more fluidly to the music now, her steps perfectly matched to those of his grandfather.

Logan couldn't help wondering—given the fact that Daniel would be the third husband of Hugh's eldest daughter, a daughter Hugh was extremely proud of but also shocked by on occasion too—exactly what the two could be finding to talk about. Whatever it was, they were obviously enjoying each other's company, laughing together several times before the music stopped and Hugh gallantly guided Darcy back to her father and Meg.

'The old devil probably enjoyed that immensely,' Brice remarked laughingly.

'Probably,' Logan acknowledged dryly. 'I think we're about to learn firsthand just how much,' he added ruefully as their grandfather made his way over to the two of them determinedly.

'What's the matter with you young men?' their grandfather attacked, helping himself to a glass of champagne as a maid passed by them with a laden tray of glasses. 'Put you amongst a lot of pretty women and you cower in a corner like a couple of idiots!' He drank the champagne thirstily.

'I take exception to the ''idiot'' part of that statement,' Brice laughed.

'And we're hardly "cowering" anywhere, Grandfather,' Logan replied.

'You aren't dancing, either.' The elderly man fixed Logan with a gaze as blue as his own. 'In fact, I haven't seen you dance once yet, Logan. What's the matter with you—company a bit too provincial for you?'

'Hardly. The majority of these people are up from London, anyway.'

'Pretty girl, that,' Hugh said appreciatively.

'Darcy?' Brice put in, his expression completely innocent as Logan turned to give him a hard glance.

'Name's a bit odd.' Hugh nodded. 'But the girl's sound enough. I suppose Meg and this Simon chap might make a match of it,' he allowed grudgingly. 'About time one of you settled down and made me a great-grandfather.' He fixed his steely gaze on both his grandsons.

'Oh, please—not you too!' Logan protested, putting his empty glass down forcefully on a side-table. 'If you'll both excuse me?'

'What did I say?' a bewildered Hugh turned to ask of Brice.

Logan didn't stay around long enough to hear Brice's reply, but strode across the room, reaching Darcy's side just ahead of one of the young actors he had been introduced to earlier.

'Dance?' Logan asked tightly.

She had turned to smile at him as he'd approached, but that smile faded as she took in his coldly angry expression. 'Are you sure that's what you want to do?' she said warily.

No, what he really wanted to do—what he wanted to do almost every time he saw Darcy!—was to carry her off somewhere and make love to her. In the circumstances, ncing with her was as close to that as he could get, so ce it would have to be.

'Perfectly sure,' he confirmed briskly.

She frowned, undecided, obviously unsure of his mood.

With good reason, Logan allowed impatiently. Damn it, he was irritable when he didn't see her, and angry most of the time when he did. He wasn't sure of his own mood at the moment!

'Perhaps you've danced enough for one evening,' he grated. 'Perhaps you would prefer to go outside for a walk, instead?'

And perhaps she wouldn't, he groaned inwardly as he saw the puzzlement on her expressive face. Would he want to go for a walk with someone who looked as frustratedly angry as he felt? Definitely not!

He drew in a deeply controlling breath. 'I'll try that again,' he said sheepishly. 'Darcy, would you care to walk outside for a breath of fresh air?'

She smiled that shy smile at him. 'Thank you, Logan. Yes, I would like that.'

He held out his arm for her to take, giving the hovering young actor a withering glare as they strolled past him, on their way to the French doors that led out onto the terrace scented with the roses his grandfather grew near the castle.

It was a beautiful moonlit evening outside, the noise of the deer close by, and nocturnal animals calling to each other in the distance, the sound of the bullfrogs nearby in the lily-pond.

'What a beautiful place this is,' Darcy murmured dreamily as she looked out over the wall, the castle, and grounds beyond, bathed in moonlight.

It was a light that seemed to reflect off the silver grey of her dress, giving the woman herself an ethereal qualit Logan found himself transfixed by her the moment t' were alone outside.

Darcy turned to give him a searching glance. 'What is it?' she breathed. 'Logan...?'

It was purely instinctive, something he had been wanting to do since the last time he had seen her, something he found himself wanting to do every time he saw her!

His arms moved about the slenderness of her waist, moulding her gently against him as his head lowered and his lips found and captured hers.

Perfect pleasure. It was the first time he had felt complete, any peace of mind, any gentleness of spirit, since the last time he had held her like this.

She fitted so perfectly against him, breathed the same air, and—he hoped!—knew the same pleasure at his closeness that he did at hers.

He wanted this never to stop, wanted to carry on kissing her, touching her, holding her—

'No!' She wrenched her mouth from his, pulling away from him, her face stricken in the moonlight. 'We can't do this, Logan,' she told him breathlessly, tears glistening in her eyes.

He was stunned for a moment, had been totally lost in the sheer pleasure of holding her close to him.

'Please let me go, Logan,' she choked, his arms having instinctively tightened like steel bands about her as she attempted to move away. 'Please!' she said again tearfully.

His hold slackened, but he still didn't release her. 'I'm not going to hurt you, Darcy,' he whispered. 'You should know by now, I would never do that.' Even under extreme provocation, all the times she had done something to him that might have resulted in retaliation, he had never so much as taken an angry step in her direction.

She became suddenly still in his arms, deliberately not king at him. 'Then let me go,' she said woodenly.

Vhy?' he groaned. 'We don't have to go back into the

salon. We can get in through one of the side doors, up to my suite of rooms—'

'No!' She wrenched out of his grasp this time, even though Logan knew it must have physically hurt her to do so. 'No, Logan…!' she choked again before turning to let herself back into the salon, the door closing softly behind her.

Logan stood there stunned for several long, dazed minutes. What had he done? What had he said? What…?

He turned sharply as he sensed a movement behind him, his disappointment acute when he saw it was Brice and not Darcy who had come outside to join him.

'Darcy came back in alone, looking nothing like her usual, calm self,' Brice informed him, 'so I thought I had better come outside and make sure she hadn't thrown you in the lily-pond!'

No, she hadn't done that. But in the last few minutes Logan knew she had done something to him much worse than that. Much, much worse than that!

How could he? How could Logan hold her, kiss her, talk of the two of them going up to his rooms together, when all the time the woman in his life, Francesca, was in the salon with all the other engagement party guests?

She had always known Logan was arrogant, a law unto himself, that he didn't believe in love, let alone marriage. But even so, she had never thought he would behave in such a cavalier fashion. In his grandfather's house, too!

What was she to do now? She couldn't stay down here, when Logan might return to the party at any moment, that was for sure. She simply couldn't face him again so soon after what had happened outside on the terrace. But neither did she want to upset her father or Meg by retiring early.

Surprisingly, it was Hugh McDonald who came to

rescue, standing up to announce it was almost midnight, that he was going to have the last waltz with the most beautiful woman in the room, and then it was time they all went to their beds or their homes.

Although Darcy wasn't so sure she had been rescued at all when his choice of the most beautiful woman in the room turned out to be her, suddenly finding herself swung expertly into his arms as the band began to play!

'Smile, you silly wee lassie,' he murmured gently in her ear as he whirled her around to *The Last Waltz*. 'Never let a McDonald know he's got you down,' he added reprovingly.

Darcy gave him a startled glance. 'A McDonald...? But you—'

'Logan's mother may have married a McKenzie, but he's more of a McDonald than any of them,' Hugh told her with a mischievous twinkle in his eye. 'A bit slow witted where the ladies are concerned, ye ken?' He gave a loud bellow of laughter at her stunned expression. 'My late wife had to hit me over the head with a frying-pan before I realised I was in love with her!'

Darcy laughed softly at the image he projected. 'I think I would like to hear that story some time!'' But she also knew that approach wouldn't work on Logan...

Darcy knew that Hugh meant well with his teasing, but she had already done too many horrific things to Logan to even think about—and all it had succeeded in doing was having him invite her upstairs to his suite of rooms. Hardly a declaration of love!

'Oh, you've tried that, have ye?' Hugh observed thoughtfully as he easily read at least some of her thoughts. 'He always was a fool where women are concerned.' He ~~hed~~. 'If I were forty years younger I'd ask ye to marry ~~myself~~.'

Darcy laughed again. 'If you were forty years younger, I think I might be tempted to accept!'

Hugh grinned down at her appreciatively as the music came to an end on the stroke of midnight, looking very much like his grandson at that moment. 'You're a refreshing addition to this family, lassie, and no mistake.' He bent down to kiss her warmly on the cheek. 'I look forward to seeing you again soon.'

At the wedding, of course. In two weeks' time. She hadn't been looking forward to it anyway, the way things were between Logan and herself, but after tonight—! Definitely not an occasion for her to look forward to!

Unfortunately, the first person she saw as she turned to leave the dance-floor was Logan, standing just inside the French doors. A glowering Logan, who stared at her with glitteringly angry blue eyes.

He was angry? He wasn't the one who had been propositioned, with his partner for the evening—night?—just on the other side of those doors!

'Isn't my father wonderful?' Meg was the one to distract her attention as she reached out and squeezed Darcy's arm affectionately, thrilled with the success the evening had obviously been.

'Wonderful,' Darcy echoed sincerely, relieved to be able to look away from that accusing blue gaze as she turned to smile at Meg and her father.

'Daniel and I are just going to have a brandy in the library before retiring. Join us,' Meg invited warmly.

Darcy shook her head. 'It's been a wonderful evening, but, like Hugh, I'm rather tired.' She moved to kiss them both warmly on the cheek. 'Why don't you ask Logan?' she suggested. 'He looks in need of a brandy.'

She didn't linger to see whether they took up her suggestion, hurrying from the room, just wanting to get aw now, desperately in need of the privacy of her bedroom. It had been a wonderful—awful, ecstatic, heart-breaking!—evening. One she hoped never to repeat.

She hesitated once out in the main hallway, presented with four sets of stairs, one presumably to each tower. Which was the one to the North Tower? That was the question.

'Are you lingering here looking helpless in the hope that Brice might turn up and offer to escort you back to your bedroom?' a hard voice scorned softly so that the other guests moving noisily past them as they left shouldn't overhear the conversation.

Darcy stiffened, steeling herself before turning to face Logan. A stony-faced Logan, his eyes glittering coldly!

What did this man want from her? More to the point, just what did he think she was? Had he really thought her capable of sneaking off with him when his girlfriend was waiting for him downstairs?

She shook her head sadly. 'I'm merely trying to decide which staircase leads to the North Tower,' she told him flatly, too tired to even attempt to deny the other accusation in his question. Brice had been kind to her, nothing more, and she wouldn't insult that kindness by trying to defend either Brice, or herself.

Logan seemed unimpressed. 'Points of the compass, Darcy,' he said tauntingly. 'East,' he pointed to one staircase. 'West.' He pointed to the one opposite. 'South—'

'Okay, Logan, I get the point,' she interrupted wearily. 'Excuse me for not being a boy scout!' Her voice broke slightly on the latter, and she turned quickly away before Logan could see the tears that had welled so quickly in her eyes, logically making her way to the staircase opposite the one that lay to the south.

'Darcy—'

'Logan, I'm so glad I found you; I've been looking for you everywhere!'

Francesca Darwin's voice was easily recognisable to Darcy as she hurried away up the wide staircase, her legs shaking so badly she wasn't sure she was going to make it.

'I've been right here,' Logan answered the other woman hardly.

Darcy managed to get to the top of the stairs before her legs gave way, turning the corner to lean weakly back against the wall, her tears starting to fall now.

She should move, she knew she should, before anyone else came up the stairs and saw her there, but her legs didn't feel capable of moving just yet. Logan hated her! There was simply no mistaking that glitter in his eyes a few minutes ago...

'I simply wanted to say how nice it's been to meet you.' Francesca was talking again now, her voice bubbling with excitement. 'It's been a wonderful evening.'

'I'm glad you enjoyed it,' Logan returned noncommittally.

Darcy was far less composed. What did the other woman mean, it had been nice meeting him...?

'Perhaps we'll meet again,' Francesca suggested.

'Perhaps,' Logan returned with clear impatience.

Darcy didn't stop to listen to any more of the conversation, moving away from the wall to stumble down the corridor to the bedroom she had been allocated on her arrival, switching on the light to close the door thankfully behind her.

She didn't understand. She had thought Francesca Darwin came here with Logan, had seen the two of them together earlier when she'd entered the salon, and had realised this had to be the woman in Logan's life. But fr the conversation she had just overheard, obviously she was wrong. And if he hadn't come here with Francesca, then it would seem he hadn't come here with anyone...

So where was the woman in his life?

If there was one, a little voice in her head reasoned. Hadn't she just assumed there had to be one? Logan had been out to lunch with someone that day ten days ago, changed his mind about being a witness at their parents' wedding, and hadn't she, Darcy, decided it had to be because of a woman's influence?

But if not another woman, what—or who!—had changed his mind?

CHAPTER THIRTEEN

WHY didn't this prattling woman just stop talking and go? Logan fumed inwardly as Francesca Darwin carried on gushing. Didn't she realise he just wasn't interested?

The only thing he was interested in was that Darcy had looked upset when she'd left him a few minutes ago, and he knew it was because of his nastiness to her. But he just couldn't seem to help himself.

Because he was in love with her...

Love. He had realised, when she'd walked away from him on the terrace earlier, that he was in love with her, that love for Darcy was the reason all the meaning had gone out of the rest of his life. It was an emotion he had thought he would never feel for any woman.

It terrified the life out of him!

Love was everything he had thought it would be: frightening, debilitating in the knowledge that all of your life's happiness was wrapped up in a single person.

But it was also many other things: exhilarating, a feeling of gladness just in that person's presence, pleasure in every movement, every word spoken, a driving need to protect, but most of all an overwhelming feeling of completeness. For the first time in his life Logan felt whole, as if he had found the other half of himself. Darcy was that other half.

It wasn't something he could choose to feel, or not, was an emotion that existed entirely of its own volition. He had never known a feeling like it, ached with love for her, f just one of those heart-stopping smiles to come his w

wanted to tell Darcy how he felt. But those feelings of
terror held him back. Because she didn't love him.

He had known that outside on the terrace too. She had
wanted to get away from him, couldn't wait to escape.

What was he going to do now?

'I'll walk you to the door, Francesca.' Brice stepped
neatly into the one-sided conversation, shooting Logan a
concerned glance before taking a firm grasp of Francesca's
arm, chatting to her amiably as they walked away.

'Logan...?'

He turned dazedly to look at his mother. Had she loved
his father in the way he now loved Darcy? Did she now
love Daniel in the same way? If she did, then he knew the
least he owed her was an apology for the way he had
treated her. Not just for months, but for years...

Meg smiled at him gently. 'Daniel and I are going to
have a brandy in the library; come and join us.' She didn't
wait for an answer, slipping her hand into the crook of his
arm as the three of them strolled to the privacy of the
library.

A fire had been lit in there, giving off a warm glow of
heat, but it was a heat that didn't touch Logan. Neither did
the glass of brandy that Daniel had pushed into his hand
and which Logan sipped distractedly.

Realising he loved Darcy, and that love wasn't returned,
was bad enough, but how did he even begin to apologise
to a mother he had repeatedly rejected over the years?

She was looking at him concernedly now. 'Logan...?'

His mother had never seen him like this before, was
obviously unsure of his mood, shooting worried glances at
Daniel as the two of them looked at Logan uncertainly.

They were probably expecting him to say or do some-
ng that would spoil their happiness, of the evening, if
ing else. And who could blame them? He had been

an idiot, a selfish idiot. He had no more right, than Darcy had quickly realised she had, to dictate what these two people should or shouldn't do with their lives.

His breath left him in a ragged sigh before he placed his brandy glass down on the table, walking over to hold out his hand to Daniel. 'I would like to offer you both my belated, warmest congratulations,' he said quietly.

To the older man's credit he only hesitated for a fraction of a second before accepting that warm handshake.

Logan turned to his mother. 'I truly hope you'll be very happy together,' he told her gruffly. 'Mamma,' he added softly.

His mother's throat moved convulsively as he used the name he'd had for her when he was a little boy. In the last twenty-one years he had only ever called her Meg, or the more condescending, Mother.

Logan reached out and hugged his mother, feeling the trembling of her body as she cried softly. Time and time again, he now acknowledged, his mother had reached out to him over the last twenty-one years, and time and time again he had repulsed her. But loving Darcy as he now did, allowing love back into the hardness of his heart, he knew he had never stopped loving his mother, that he never could or would.

'You've made me so happy, Logan,' his mother choked, cradling his face in both her hands as she reached up and gently kissed him on the cheek.

'Just be happy together, hmm?' he encouraged huskily.

'And you?' His mother looked up at him searchingly. 'Are you happy, Logan?'

'If I'm not, I have only myself to blame,' he replie ruefully.

He had chosen to live the way that he did, had hard

his heart to love; there was no one else to blame if he now found himself alone.

'Darcy—'

'Is a beautiful and charming young lady,' Logan cut in on Daniel's tentative remark, steadily meeting the older man's gaze.

Did Daniel know? Had Logan given himself away somehow? Had his feelings for Darcy been so obvious to everyone but himself…? Did Darcy know?

'She's a credit to you, Daniel,' he added flatly, dismayed at the thought of Darcy guessing how he felt about her. Was that the reason she had run away from him…?

Daniel's arm was about Meg's shoulders now. 'I'm not so sure about the time she threw egg-white over you,' he mused affectionately.

Logan shrugged. 'I probably deserved it. At least she's honest in her feelings.'

Something he hadn't been in a long time. And wasn't it about time that he was? Completely honest. No matter what the cost to his personal pride?

He straightened. 'If you don't mind, I think I'll leave the two of you alone now. What a stupid thing to say; of course you don't mind being left alone.' He shook his head at his own ridiculousness. 'Just take care of my mother, Daniel,' he asked.

Daniel's arm tightened about Meg's shoulders. 'Depend on it.'

Strange, but Logan had a feeling as he left the older couple alone together that he could do exactly that. None of them knew what was round the corner for them, as his mother hadn't when his father had died so suddenly, leaving her bereft and vulnerable. As he hadn't when he'd n in love with Darcy…

It took him only a few minutes to find out what he wanted to know, before making his way upstairs.

But there was no answer when he knocked on Darcy's bedroom door. She must already be asleep.

What he wanted to say would have to wait until morning. Why not? It had waited thirty-five years, another night wasn't going to kill him! Or, at least, he hoped it wasn't! A sleepless night was probably the least he could expect. He only hoped he didn't lose his nerve overnight!

It was the shock of his life when he rounded the corner at the top of the South Tower stairs and found Darcy walking along the corridor towards him. Not tucked up in bed asleep at all, but still dressed in that clinging grey dress.

And she looked stricken as she looked up and saw him!

If he dared—if he made one rude remark about her being here—

'Darcy,' he greeted lightly. 'Did you get lost, after all?'

He didn't sound rude, or sarcastic…

But that was no guarantee that he wasn't going to be. He—

'Would you like me to show you back to your bedroom?' he offered gently.

Darcy continued to eye him warily. 'Er—actually, I—my father and Meg invited me to join them for a brandy in the library, I couldn't sleep, so I thought I might join them, after all.'

Coward, she instantly berated herself. She could hardly have expected to find the library in the South Tower! But her courage had completely deserted her at coming face to face with Logan unexpectedly like this.

Logan nodded. 'I've just left them. I…think they woul probably like to be alone for a while now.'

'Of course.' There was embarrassed colour in her cheeks now. 'How silly of me.'

'How about joining me in the family sitting-room for a brandy, instead?' he suggested. 'I would like to talk to you, anyway,' he elaborated as she was about to refuse.

Darcy's confusion returned a hundredfold. She had felt she owed Logan an explanation for her behaviour on the terrace after realising her misunderstanding concerning Francesca earlier, had bullied herself into going in search of Logan to make that apology this evening, knowing she would never sleep if she didn't. But her relief had been immense when she'd knocked, on what she had found out from one of the maids was his bedroom door, and he hadn't answered. Now she knew it was because he had been downstairs with her father and Meg.

But didn't she still owe him that explanation...?

'Thank you,' she accepted awkwardly, accompanying him down the stairs.

The family sitting-room was much less formal than the rooms she had seen so far, a warm fire burning in the grate, old comfortable furniture, books and magazines lying around, family photographs everywhere. No doubt some of them would be of Logan when he was a boy. Darcy ached to be able to go and look at them.

'Here.' Logan held out a glass of brandy to her.

She took the glass, gingerly sipping the fiery liquid. Dutch courage, she inwardly taunted herself. 'Logan—'

'Let's sit down, hmm.' He indicated the over-stuffed sofa behind them, waiting until she was seated before sitting down next to her.

Instantly throwing Darcy into confusion again. Being near Logan at any time was torture for her, but with him in this strange, unfathomable mood, she found it even more difficult to bear.

He watched the brandy as he swirled it around in his glass. 'I thought you would like to know I've made my peace with my mother,' he told her softly.

'You have?' She breathed emotionally, unbidden tears springing into her eyes. 'Oh, Logan, that's wonderful!' And she meant it. Logan might not appreciate it yet, but it would be better for him too not to have that awkwardness in his life.

'I have.' He nodded, looking up suddenly, his gaze blazing into hers. 'And now I would like to make my peace with you.'

Darcy sat back slightly. 'With me...?' She frowned.

He sighed, nodding again. 'If I frightened or upset you earlier when we were outside—'

'Oh, but you didn't,' she instantly protested. Fear was the last thing she had felt in his arms earlier!

'I didn't?' He looked bemused. 'Well, no matter.' He shrugged. 'I obviously did something wrong. And for that I apologise. The last thing I ever want to do is frighten or upset you.'

Darcy was suddenly aware of the grandfather clock ticking behind them, of the silence in the castle after the noise of the party earlier. She was also aware that whatever came next had to come from her.

'You didn't do either of those things, Logan.' She chewed on her inner lip. 'I—I thought Francesca Darwin was your—I believed she was staying here. At the castle. With you!' The words came tumbling out.

Logan looked back at her uncomprehendingly. 'Why on earth should you have thought that?' he finally said slowly.

Darcy stood up, moving away from him. She couldn't think straight sitting close to him like that! 'She was wit' you when Brice and I joined you. She sat next to you dinner. And you changed your mind about being a wit'

at the wedding after lunch that day!' she continued determinedly.

Logan looked as if he was trying to make sense of what
she was saying.

'It was obvious that whoever it was you had lunch with
ten days ago had helped change your mind,' Darcy went
on frustratedly.

'You're right. They did.' He pursed his lips. 'And you
believed it had to be a woman?'

'Of course it—you mean it wasn't?' Darcy looked at
him uncertainly.

Logan shook his head. 'It was Fergus. Although a
woman was indirectly involved in my change of mind,' he
admitted.

Darcy sighed heavily. 'I thought so.'

Logan put down his own brandy glass to stand up, only
inches away from her again now. 'That woman was you,
Darcy,' he told her gruffly.

Her eyes widened. 'Me? But—'

He sighed. 'Fergus and Brice were both going to be at
the wedding. They are both incredibly attractive to women,
consummate flirts. And you—'

She held her breath, willing him to go on. And when
he didn't, 'I what, Logan?' she prompted.

He took a deep breath. 'Darcy, what were you really
doing wandering around the South Tower just now?'

'Looking for you,' she admitted. 'I overheard Francesca
talking to you as she left, realised what a terrible mistake
I had made concerning the two of you. I—needed to tell
you that.'

'Why?'

'Because!' she said. 'I what, Logan?' she pushed again.

He seemed to be fighting an inner battle with himself,

finally giving a deep sigh, before smiling at her. 'You are bright, funny, beautiful, charming, sexy—'

'Logan—'

'And so I decided I had to come to the wedding after all, so that one of those two charming bastards didn't walk away with the woman I love!' he finished.

Darcy stared at him, swallowing convulsively, sure she couldn't have heard him correctly. Logan loved her? But he didn't believe in love. He had said so. Hadn't he…?

'Now I really have shocked you,' he realised with pained self-revelation.

She hesitated. 'I'm not shocked: I—you really do love me?' she said uncertainly, her heart threatening to burst inside her chest.

'I really do,' he confirmed. 'I can imagine nothing more wonderful than waking up with you beside me for the rest of my life, having you to talk with, to laugh with, to cry with, if necessary. I wouldn't even mind if you felt the occasional urge to throw egg-white over me.'

Darcy was still staring at him disbelievingly. 'I—did you know that your grandmother hit your grandfather over the head with a frying-pan in an attempt to get him to realise he was in love with her?'

He looked stunned. 'My sweet ladylike grandmother did?'

Darcy nodded. 'Apparently.'

'Did it work? Obviously it did; they were happily married for over fifty years,' he ruefully answered his own question before looking up at her sharply. 'Darcy, are you trying to tell me, in your own inimitable style, that you did those things to me because you love me?'

She laughed breathlessly. 'Not exactly. Oh, not becau I don't love you,' she quickly assured him as he loo

suddenly ravaged. 'I just didn't realise then that was the
reason you made me so angry all the time.'

Logan was the one to look unsure of himself now. Not
an emotion Darcy particularly associated with him, admittedly. And not one she particularly like seeing, either.

She took a step towards him, only inches away from
him now. 'Logan McKenzie, I am very much in love with
you,' she told him shakily.

'Darcy Simon, I am very much in love with you too,'
he returned shyly, his hands reaching out to grasp her
shoulders. 'Will you marry me?'

She took a deep breath. 'Marriage, Logan? Don't you
want to get used to the idea of being in love first?' she
attempted to tease, although her voice broke emotionally.

'No,' he said with certainty. 'I don't ever want to get
used to this feeling. It's wonderful. Exhilarating.' His
hands tightened on her arms as he bent slightly to gently
kiss her on the mouth, that kiss quickly deepening into
passion.

Darcy had no idea how long they were in each other's
arms, kissing, touching, discovering. It was wonderful!

'I think I fell in love with you that very first day,' Logan
finally admitted, his forehead resting against hers as the
two of them sat close together on the sofa, their arms about
each other.

'I don't believe that,' Darcy responded, resting against
his chest. 'I cried all over you. And I looked a mess.'

Logan chuckled throatily. 'Your tears are what make
you so human, Darcy. As for your smile—it takes my
breath away. Will you marry me?'

'Oh, yes,' she breathed ecstatically, unable to imagine
anything more wonderful than being with Logan for the
rest of their lives.

'Soon?' he urged achingly.

'Very soon,' she acquiesced, knowing she wanted nothing more than to belong with this man for the rest of her life. She chuckled softly. 'I still can't believe this, Logan.' She cuddled into him. 'I promise I'll never kick you or throw egg-white over you again—'

'Don't promise things you can't keep to, my love.' Logan laughed. 'I'm sure I'll occasionally do things that will annoy you, and you'll react instinctively. I love your unpredictability, Darcy. In fact, I'm quite expecting you to present me with twins—possibly even triplets!—one day, as your pièce de résistance!'

What a wonderful thought!

In fact, the future, with Logan, promised to be full of wonderful things...

Modern Romance™
...seduction and
passion guaranteed

Tender Romance™
...love affairs that
last a lifetime

Sensual Romance™
...sassy, sexy and
seductive

Blaze
...sultry days and
steamy nights

Medical Romance™
...medical drama on
the pulse

Historical Romance™
...rich, vivid and
passionate

MILLS & BOON®

Winner at

2001 IDEA INTERNATIONAL
DESIGN
EFFECTIVENESS
AWARDS

MIRANDA LEE

Secrets & Sins

revealed

SEDUCED BY HER BODYGUARD AND STALKED BY A STRANGER...

Available from 15th March 2002

Available at most branches of WH Smith, Tesco, Martins, Borders, Eason, Sainsbury's and most good paperback bookshops.

SANDRA MARTON

raising the stakes

When passion is a gamble...

Available from 19th April 2002

*Available at most branches of WH Smith,
Tesco, Martins, Borders, Eason, Sainsbury's
and most good paperback bookshops.*

0502/135/MB35

2 FREE

books and a surprise gift!

We would like to take this opportunity to thank you for reading this Mills & Boon® book by offering you the chance to take TWO more specially selected titles from the Modern Romance™ series absolutely FREE! We're also making this offer to introduce you to the benefits of the Reader Service™—:

★ FREE home delivery
★ FREE gifts and competitions
★ FREE monthly Newsletter
★ Exclusive Reader Service discount
★ Books available before they're in the shops

Accepting these FREE books and gift places you under no obligation to buy, you may cancel at any time, even after receiving your free shipment. Simply complete your details below and return the entire page to the address below. *You don't even need a stamp!*

YES! Please send me 2 free Modern Romance books and a surprise gift. I understand that unless you hear from me, I will receive 4 superb new titles every month for just £2.55 each, postage and packing free. I am under no obligation to purchase any books and may cancel my subscription at any time. The free books and gift will be mine to keep in any case.

P2ZEA

Ms/Mrs/Miss/Mr ....Initials...............................
BLOCK CAPITALS PLEASE

Surname ....

Address ....

....

....Postcode...............................

Send this whole page to:
UK: FREEPOST CN81, Croydon, CR9 3WZ
EIRE: PO Box 4546, Kilcock, County Kildare (stamp required)